"What a lovely night," Damaris murmured.

No woman, his lordship thought dazedly, had the right to have eyes as black as midnight and lips as soft as a pomegranate flower.

"Yes," he agreed. "Lovely."

His voice was husky, his face lined against the dark. In the shadows, his hard profile softened, and the line of his mouth was tender. The expression in his eyes made Damaris catch her breath.

She knew that he was going to kiss her. She wanted him to. Damaris closed her eyes as his lordship lowered his lips to hers. All she could feel was the firm, sweet pressure of his lips on hers.

Then into this magical world intruded a thundering, explosive noise. There were shrieks and howls of "It's them anarchists!" and "Murder!" and one man insisted that Napoleon had come back to invade England.

Damaris pulled free of Lord Sinclair's arms.

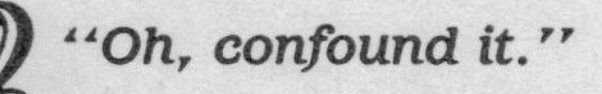

"Oh, confound it."

Also by Rebecca Ward
Published by Fawcett Books:

FAIR FORTUNE
LORD LONGSHANKS
LADY IN SILVER
CINDERELLA'S STEPMOTHER
ENCHANTED RENDEZVOUS

MADAM MYSTERY

Rebecca Ward

FAWCETT CREST • NEW YORK

A Fawcett Crest Book
Published by Ballantine Books
 Published in the United States by Ballantine Books, a division of Random House, Inc., New York, and simultaneously in Canada by Random House of Canada Limited, Toronto.

Library of Congress Catalog Card Number: 91-75840

ISBN 0-449-22054-0

Manufactured in the United States of America

First Edition: March 1992

For Ellen K. Gould

Chapter One

Sussex looked best in harvest gold. Lord Sinclair was conscious of the landscape's cheerful warmth, so at variance with his own mood, as he drove his curricle through his uncle's estate and up to Pardom Hall.

"My uncle in, Murton?" he inquired of the distinguished butler who answered the door.

"You will find the earl in the study, m'lord—" But Murton's words were interrupted by a bloodcurdling scream. With an oath, Sinclair strode through the ground-floor anteroom, took the stairs two at a time, and ran across the second-floor landing to fling open the study door.

"What the devil!" he exclaimed.

Molyneux Beekley, fifth Earl of Pardom, was lying on the floor. A dagger with a ruby hilt protruded from his chest.

The earl's valet had one leg thrown over the sill of the study window. No doubt the blackguard was attempting to escape. Sinclair flung himself across the room and, catching the man by the lapels of his jacket, hauled him back into the room.

"Now, you scoundrel," he gritted.

"Curst young idiot!" The earl had sat up and was glaring balefully at his nephew. "Who asked you to interfere? Ruined everything."

He removed the dagger from his shirtfront and flung it petulantly aside. "Yibberly and I were enacting the murder scene from *Lord Tedell's Revenge.*"

For a moment Lord Sinclair stared. Then he gave a crack of laughter and released the valet, who bowed deeply and with such offended dignity that his lordship laughed even harder.

"Oh, go away, Yibberly," Pardom said grumpily. "And you help me up," he added to his nephew. "Curse you, anyway. You know how Yibberly is. He'll be glumping and sulking for the next week, thanks to you."

Sinclair complied, settled into a cane-backed chair, stretched out his long legs, and demanded, "So you've taken to enacting rubbishy novels, have you, Uncle?"

The earl's large, stout form quivered as if he had received a mortal blow. His square face turned a shade more florid, his red-rimmed eyes narrowed. "I'll thank you to keep a civil tongue in your head," he growled. "Desmond Winter don't write rubbish. His books are regular goers. Got action in 'em, and suspense."

"And murder and mayhem and a brilliant fellow who catches the evildoers in the end," Sinclair remarked dryly. "Yes, I know. You've told me all about them."

"Lord Tedell *is* curst clever. You should read one of Winter's novels, Nicholas, before you start scoffing. What're you here for, anyway?"

Sinclair regarded his relative impatiently. "You sent for me. You said you wanted to talk to me."

"So I did." The earl rocked back on his heels. "Want your opinion on something. Got to think for a moment first."

Sinclair leaned back into his chair and looked idly about the study. It was a thoroughly masculine room, unfashionably furnished with the earl's faded hunt scenes, ancient but comfortable furniture, and dog-eared books. On the cluttered table beside Sinclair's chair lay a book by Desmond Winter, jars of snuff, and the latest edition of the *Gentleman's Magazine*. Beside the magazine stood a bowl of autumn flowers.

"Liza's new governess brought 'em in," complained the earl. "Makes me sneeze. Told her to pitch 'em out and the wretched woman started wailing and sobbing till you'd have thought I'd murdered her. That's females for you, Nicholas."

He reached for the nearest jar of snuff, shook back a pinch, sneezed violently, and resumed, "My late countess was a good woman. A curst good woman, in fact. But she disappointed me, Nicholas. Pardom needed a son—and she had to present me with Liza. Shows a serious lack of family feeling."

Sinclair suggested that perhaps the lady could not help it.

"Well, she should have done," continued his aggrieved relative. "Deuced queer stirrups I find myself in now, I can tell you. Here I am, one of the warmest men in the county without a proper heir. Oh, I know that the title goes to you, but I'd like to leave my blunt to someone besides a chuckleheaded, provoking creature like my daughter."

Even more impatiently, Sinclair asked, "Did you bring me all the way from Hampshire just to tell me that?"

"No, that ain't it. I've written to Desmond Winter."

"To this fool of a writer, you mean?"

The earl's eyes narrowed still further. He was fond of his late brother's only son, who, he was wont to tell himself when he was on the mop and in a sentimental mood, was like the son he had never had. Pardom had seen Nicholas grow from a puling creature in leading strings to a handsome fellow of six feet and more, as strong an athlete as ever donned gloves at Gentleman Jim's, and a brave officer who had—mercifully—survived years of war which had taken the lives of many of his friends.

Yes, he was fond of this nephew of his, but these days he did not understand what went on in Nicholas's brain box. He had always been full of frisk, a bruising rider to hounds and the sort of man to whom all others turned because he exuded warmth and humor and understanding. Men found him the best of friends; the ladies fluttered when he bent over their hands; noted hostesses had prized him as a vastly eligible gentleman who could be relied upon to be as attentive to the dowdiest squab as to the most peerless heiress.

Pardom sighed. All this was in the past. Since his return from Waterloo, Nicholas had changed.

He had not, upon selling his colors, gone to the dogs as so many others had, nor did he racket around London or fritter his blunt away. Pardom felt that he could have understood these things. Instead, Nicholas had ignored his fashionable London town house and avoided society. He had rusticated on his Hampshire estate until he was in danger of becoming a recluse. His humor had become cynical, his laughter sardonic, his tongue sharp, until he could be curst uncomfortable company.

And now Nicholas was ridiculing Desmond Winter. "I wouldn't make fun of him," the earl growled.

"He's a curst fine writer and a clever one. I've sent a letter to his publishers in London and asked them to forward a letter to him. Asked him to come to Pardom."

Absently Lord Sinclair rubbed the healed scar on his forearm. "Was it necessary to invite that fribble *here*?" he wondered.

"He ain't fribble," the earl shouted. Then, controlling himself with an effort, he added, "The long and short of it is that I've made him an offer. If he comes here and writes a book about Pardom Hall, I told Winter I'd pay him four plums."

His nephew's lip curled. "I suppose that you mean to be the hero of this little piece?"

"Well, why shouldn't I be? I'll be paying for it. Of course," the earl continued judiciously, "I'm not such a flat as to let Winter use my name—or my property's neither, so you needn't worry that I'll be a seven-day wonder. Think of it, my boy. A Desmond Winter yarn about Pardom. And me! It boggles the imagination."

Reflecting that fools and their money were soon parted, Sinclair shrugged. "Can you vouch for Winter's honesty?" he drawled. "Or do we have him turn out his pockets before he leaves?"

Pardom scowled and said that of course the man was no thief.

"No doubt he's as honest as that blackguard who had you invest in nonexistent diamond mines. Or the fellow who convinced you that there was gold buried in the east pasture and then made off with the family silver. Think about it, Uncle. And while you're at it, consider Liza—"

The earl interrupted to announce that his daughter was the last thing he desired to consider. "Well, you should," Sinclair exclaimed with some energy. "This Winter might be a Captain Sharp or a gazetted fortune hunter."

"Slum," the earl snorted. "The chit's seventeen—barely out of the schoolroom. Besides, he won't notice her. Be busy writing."

Sinclair retreated into ennui. "Why consult me if your mind's made up?"

"Because you're a downy one" was the prompt reply. "Curse it, I trust your judgment. I may have been on the short side of a take-in from time to time, and— Look here, Nicholas, I want you to meet Winter. Let me know what you think of the man."

Lord Sinclair reflected briefly on a paragraph his uncle had insisted on reading to him, a paragraph that had described Winter's hero, Horatio, Lord Tedell. Apparently Lord Tedell outwitted evildoers and caused flutters in the hearts of beautiful women. He was handsome and always dressed in the crack of fashion. He was never wrong, he never lost his nerve or his temper, and he always said exactly the right thing at the right time.

In short, Tedell was insufferable. No doubt Desmond Winter was just as repulsive.

"Mind, I want your *honest* opinion based on facts," the earl was saying. "Don't want to be made a fool of, after all."

Which meant that he would have to spend some time visiting Sussex and waste boring evenings with this author of mediocre novels. If he did not have a genuine affection for his uncle, Sinclair reflected dismally, he would wash his hands of the whole foolish business. But he could not allow his flesh and blood to be victimized by an opportunist.

No matter how tiresome it proved to be, he would have to keep an eye on his sheep-brained relative and make sure that he was not dipped too deeply by Mr. Desmond Winter.

* * *

"You must forgive my surprise, Miss Cardell. I had no idea that Mr. Winter was so charming a lady."

Damaris smiled ruefully as the tall blond gentleman in the fashionable plum-colored coat and natty dove-colored breeches bowed over her hand. "Alas, Mr. Garland, not even my publishers are aware of that fact."

"Your secret is safe with me." Ambrose Garland bestowed a respectful squeeze on Damaris's small, ink-stained hand before letting it go. "But I confess to being puzzled, ma'am. You write so well about diversions usually unfamiliar to ladies."

The high-nosed, gray-haired lady by the window looked up from her sewing to click her tongue repressively. "Like cockfighting and curricle racing, you mean? I have often told you, Damaris, that a description of such subjects is unsuited to a daughter of the late Sir Everard Cardell."

"But not to Desmond Winter," Damaris pointed out equably. "And since Lord Tedell has many adventures, I must research his world."

The dowager Lady Cardell sniffed. "That means, Mr. Garland, that my granddaughter sends her younger brother and the gardener to ask questions for her. Research, indeed. It's well enough to amuse yourself, my gel, but you must remember that you are a lady."

Ladies needed to eat, too. As she watched her ladyship select thread for her embroidery, Damaris was torn between affection and exasperation. Unlike Grandpapa, who knew full well that the wolf was at the door, Grandmama still insisted on pretending that the Cardells were a plump-pursed family.

She listened as Mr. Garland cast oil on troubled waters by asking the old lady about her school days. He was apparently the grandson of one of Lady

Cardell's girlhood friends, and since business had brought him to Kent, he had called to convey his grandmother's greetings.

Damaris glanced surreptitiously at the battered ormolu clock on the mantel and wondered how much longer Mr. Garland's visit would last. She did not object to him, for he was quite handsome and had pleasant manners, but it was close to noon. Soon she would be obliged to invite him to lunch.

Rising to her feet, Damaris said, "I collect that you have much to speak of, so I will leave you to have a good cose in peace."

Lady Cardell nodded. "Thank you, my dear. And should you see Peter, send him up to meet Mr. Garland and hear about his adventures on the peninsula. No doubt the boy is riding his horse and does not know we have a visitor."

The only horse left in the stables was Old Mope, who was too slow and ancient to be sold. As for Peter, he was chopping wood in the back. All of which Grandmama knew, of course.

"And inform Hepzibah to set another place for luncheon," my lady continued grandly. "No, no, my dear boy, I insist upon it. You must meet Cardell—he is a man of science, you know—and the other grandchildren."

As he made graceful assent, Garland registered the fact that Miss Cardell did not want him to stay for lunch. He watched her as she walked across the faded carpet, admired the straight line of her back, and found himself wondering how she would look in something other than her twice-turned morning dress of withered-leaf brown. She was hardly a beauty, with a too thin face and serious black eyes, but her hair was truly magnificent—so dark an auburn that inky lights seemed to shift in it when she moved. He judged her to be in her middle twenties, which meant she was fast leaving her youth behind.

A pity, Garland reflected, for Damaris Cardell had nothing to tempt a suitor. The old lady's pretensions notwithstanding, one look around the threadbare room with its patched curtains, cracked window frames, and ancient furniture had told him that Miss Cardell did not write to amuse herself. She wrote to pay the bills.

The Cardells might come from good stock, but just now they seemed badly dipped. Wryly Garland wondered what would be served at luncheon.

What could they give the man to eat? Damaris gnawed on the problem as she left the morning room and walked down the long staircase hall. Once this hall had been brave with silk hangings and statues by John Cheere, and there had been fine paintings on the wall. Now the statues had long since been sold, the silk hangings had been cannibalized to make dresses, undergarments, and sheets, and the artwork had been carted away and pawned. Only one painting remained—a portrait of a lady in a blue ball dress. Damaris paused at the top of the stairs to look up at it and smile.

"Hello, Mama," she whispered.

The lady smiled sweetly back at her, and Damaris felt a lift of heart. It was a private ritual she had begun five years ago when Lady Linda had died shortly after giving birth to Belle.

That year had marked the first time grief had come to Cardell House, and like an unwelcome guest, grief had stayed. Apparently a brooding melancholy had unhinged Sir Everard's good sense and caused him to be rash in his speculations. In a matter of months there was nothing left of the Cardell's fortune, and Sir Everard had shot himself.

Then there had been the horrible business of disposing of all the estate that was not entailed, and the removal of all the servants except for old Bowens, the gardener, and Hepzibah, the cook-housekeeper. And finally, just when they thought they were turning the corner, Edward had been killed at Waterloo.

"There you are, Miss Damaris," a nasal voice exclaimed. A tall, sharp-boned woman in a starched apron and frilled white cap had come up the stairs. "Is the man staying to lunch, then?" she asked. "God save us in the day of disaster. There's not enough soup, and the bread has got mold on it."

Damaris bore this recital without flinching. Hepzibah McPhree had been with the family for nearly thirty years, and her small eyes saw doom everywhere.

"Isn't there trouble enough already?" Hepzibah continued mournfully. "What with his lordship locking himself into the stables with that horrid machine of his, and that puir, wee lad chopping wood as though he was no better than a servant. He will be cutting off his foot, I am thinking."

Damaris glanced out the landing window and saw her brother Peter chopping wood so hard that his red head bobbed up and down. Peter was only twelve, but he was now the man of the family, and he took his duties seriously.

Unfortunately, he was also at that ungainly age when he seemed always to be tripping over his own feet. God send he did not do himself an injury with the ax, Damaris thought, but she knew that she could do nothing about it. Bowens was too arthritic even to lift the ax, and the family needed wood for the cookstove.

"Water the soup and wipe the bread clean of mold," she advised. "Mr. Garland will not mind rough fare, Hepzibah. He has been a soldier and has served on the peninsula."

Hepzibah's eyes filled with tears. "Och, ochon, like puir Master Edward. It is the way of this cruel world, entirely."

Requesting that the meal be served at once, Damaris went outside to call the children. Peter, red-faced from chopping, told her he would be in as soon as he finished a few more logs, and Harriet was with the younger children in the overgrown rose garden. While making a cornhusk doll for Belle, she was listening to the twins read their lesson—an adventure story that Damaris had written for them.

They broke off as Damaris came up to them and Harriet asked, wistfully, "Must we have soup again, Dami?"

Harriet was only sixteen, but her hazel eyes were old for her years. She was the prettiest of the Cardells, with her curly strawberry blond hair and a deep dimple in her chin. Looking at her, Damaris wished suddenly and fiercely that she could afford to buy a new dress for her sister and a come-out party that would make Hetty the toast of the ton.

"I am afraid so," she said. "But there is a surprise, Hetty. A gentleman has come to lunch with us, and he is vastly entertaining. Lancelot, he has been a soldier on the peninsula—and he told Grandmama that he has traveled about the continent. Would you not like to hear his stories, Fiona? Then go with Hetty. You too, darling Belle."

"You would make an excellent general, Miss Cardell."

Damaris saw that Ambrose Garland had followed her into the garden. "Lady Cardell sent me out to find you," he explained. "It seems as though luncheon is ready."

He was looking about him as he spoke, and Damaris could see the pity in his handsome blue eyes. Pride stiffened her spine and her voice as she declared, "Then we better go in. I beg you excuse me, I must call my grandfather to table."

Hauteur and noblesse oblige—in her way, Garland reflected, the country miss was more of a grand lady than her grandmother. He watched with some interest as Damaris knocked on the stable door and cried, "Grandpapa, please leave off what you are doing and come to lunch."

The door creaked open, and Lord Cardell pushed his face through the crack. His sparse gray hair stood up in tufts across his head, his long face was streaked with grease, and the eyes behind thick-lensed glasses were belligerent.

"Go away," he ordered.

"But you must eat to keep up your strength," Damaris protested.

Lord Cardell uttered a rude sound and said that he was not so bacon-brained as to think that any strength could be found in the soup Hepzibah was serving up for the third consecutive time. "You won't like it, neither," he advised Mr. Garland. "Tastes like dishwater. Tastes worse, come to think of it. 'Struth! Besides, I'm busy."

The stable door closed with a bang. "What is he doing in there?" Garland asked curiously.

"He *says* that he is creating something called the Wonder, but he will tell us nothing about it. I will have to bring his food to him." Resignedly Damaris turned away from the stable. "We had better return to the house—unless you have changed your mind about the soup."

All the family except Peter and old Lord Cardell were awaiting them at table. "Usually the children have their meals in the nursery," Lady Cardell explained regally, "but today is a special occasion. Very well, Hepzibah. You may serve."

But instead of soup, the bony woman was carrying an envelope. "For Miss Damaris," she said darkly. "A mannie brought it just now from that there Lunnon."

Damaris felt a swell of relief. A letter from London could only mean that the firm of Dane and Palchard had accepted her latest novel and was sending her their usual fee. She opened the envelope and then exclaimed, "But this is a letter from the Earl of Pardom."

"An earl!" Harriet exclaimed, and the twins craned their necks to see the letter. "How does he know you, Dami?"

Damaris hastily scanned the letter. "According to this, the earl wrote my publishers, who forwarded his wafer to me. He professes himself to be an avid reader of the adventures of Lord Tedell and says that he particularly enjoyed *Lord Tedell's Revenge*. He says—"

Damaris broke off, put down the letter, and regarded her family with a bemused expression. "He wants Mr. Desmond Winter to write a Lord Tedell novel revolving about him and his estate."

Garland favored her with a keen look. "I felicitate you," he exclaimed. "Your fortune is made, ma'am. Once the ton discovers Desmond Winter, his books will be in great demand."

"There is more," Damaris interrupted. "The earl continues that in order to have a 'feel' for his estate, he wishes 'Mr. Winter' to come and work at Pardom Hall."

"But that is not possible!" Lady Cardell exclaimed.

Harriet had risen from her place at the table and was peering over Damaris's shoulder. "The earl writes that he and his daughter would welcome Mr. Winter as a guest. Grandmama, since he has a daughter in residence, it would be quite proper for Dami to reside at Pardom Hall."

"Proper—and profitable," Damaris amended.

"The earl is offering me four hundred pounds to write the book."

The hush that descended upon the table was broken by a huzzah from Lancelot. Hepzibah almost smiled. Fiona began to pound the table with her spoon. Belle clapped her hands, and Harriet gasped, "Dami—four hundred pounds. That is a fortune! I can hardly credit it!"

Damaris jumped up and hugged her sister. "I can't believe it either," she confessed. She was aware that Mr. Garland was watching her with an odd expression in his eyes, but she was too happy to care what he thought. Four hundred pounds would make all the difference in the world.

"Stop this nonsense at once!" Lady Cardell had risen, a hand dramatically pressed to her heart. "It cannot be," she intoned. "Remember, Damaris, that you are a lady."

Striving to keep the impatience from her voice, Damaris said, "Grandmama, we cannot afford to turn away four hundred pounds."

"You mistake me," Lady Cardell declared. "I mean that you are a female. The Earl of Pardom is a hopeless misogynist. He would never countenance a woman writer."

There was another silence, broken by Damaris, who cried, "How do you know this?"

"The earl kept a town house in London, on Mount Street, not too far from ours. We were invited to many of the same parties and routs and musicals. The countess was a sweet-tempered lady, and their little daughter was an appealing infant—a year or so older than Harriet, I believe her to be. But Pardom!"

The dowager's bosom seemed to swell with outrage. "The man was the outside of enough. A bad-tempered, toplofty sapskull, who bullied his wife and made it plain that he considered females inferior. Why, he once had the barefaced gall to call me—*me*—a sour-faced squeeze crab. I hear," Lady Cardell added viciously, "that his countess died some years back. It must have been a happy release."

Damaris listened with a sinking heart. If her grandmother was correct, the earl would rescind his offer the moment he discovered the true identity of "Desmond Winter." In fact, he would probably never read another Lord Tedell novel.

Harriet had been watching her older sister's face. "Is there nothing that can be done?"

"Alas, no. Not unless I can find a gentleman willing to pose as Mr. Winter."

She had spoken lightly to cover her own deep disappointment with a jest. Damaris was surprised when Mr. Garland said, "For the sake of argument, suppose that you could find such a person?"

He was helping her bring the conversation around to a lighter level, and she was grateful. "Well, then, I imagine that this fictitious gentleman could present himself as Mr. Winter while I—the real writer—pretended to be his secretary."

"Better to pretend to be his sister as well," Harriet suggested seriously. "It would be more proper that way."

"Very well, his sister. And . . . But this is all a bag of moonshine, of course. Hepzibah, will you serve the soup?"

A yell of pain, muffled by distance and the windowpane, interrupted her. Damaris jumped to her feet and, running to the window, saw her brother clutching his left arm.

"Peter!" she screamed. "Oh, he *has* hurt himself!"

She picked up her skirts and ran out of the room, raced down the hall, and nearly tumbled down the steps in her hurry to get outside. She was fleet of foot, but before she had reached the outer door, Ambrose Garland had outstripped her.

She found him standing over Peter and examining his arm. "All's well, Miss Cardell," he called cheerfully. "The ax nicked your brother's arm, that's all."

"It's nothing," Peter growled. Embarrassment had made his face almost as red as his hair. "You're a proper widgeon, Dami, to kick up such a lot of dust over a scratch."

Damaris wanted to hug her brother. She wanted to shake him. She looked down at her feet and saw the wood that he had been chopping, and the old lump returned to her throat.

Speaking around it as best she could, she said, "You have nearly scared me to death. Make your bow to Mr. Garland, you wretched boy."

Peter bowed stiffly, but before he could speak, there was a terrible roar from the stables. A puff of black smoke belched out of the door, and Lord Cardell came catapulting out onto the grass.

His lordship was black from head to toe. His clothes looked as though they had been thrown on during a storm. His spectacles hung on the edge of his sharp nose, and he pushed them back while wheezing, "A minor mishap. Damned valves stuck again. Slight error in my calculations. 'Struth! Know what to do next time."

He picked himself up and limped back into the stables. "Next time he might blow up the place," Garland exclaimed.

"I know," she muttered.

"Perhaps Lord Cardell is so anxious to succeed because of a lack of funds."

"There is no 'perhaps' about it," Damaris said bluntly. "I am sure you have guessed by now that we are beside the bridge."

"Then why not accept the earl's offer?"

For a moment she stared at him. "You are joking me," she then said. "You cannot mean—"

"I'm bored with my life in London, and my business in Kent is over. To impersonate an author might be an amusing experience. Besides, you would do all the actual work."

He spoke so reasonably that for an instant the thing actually seemed possible. But then reality came flooding back. It would take at least a month to write a book, and no man in his right mind would agree to spend so long a time on an "amusing experience."

"As I have said, my business here is concluded, and I'm in no hurry to return to London." Dryly, Garland found himself reflecting on the various reasons why he was not anxious to return to that city. "Truth to tell, I miss the dash and excitement of my days on the peninsula. Nor am I a stranger to disguise. Often, for the sake of a jest, I would slip over to the French side dressed as a Frog."

It was tempting—but it was mad, too. And there was another consideration. Damaris asked herself what a man like Mr. Garland could want in return for his assistance.

As if he had read her mind, he smiled reassuringly. "I am entirely at your disposal, Miss Cardell. No need to insult me by suggesting that you, ah, share the earl's largess with me. Being of use to you and your family is enough reward. That and the humor of the thing."

The pittance that her publishers paid her would hardly keep the family afloat. Unless she found some cash and soon, Lord Cardell would undoubtedly be spurred on to greater disasters. And next time Peter might truly be hurt. With a sinking heart, Damaris knew that she really had few options open to her.

"Well, Miss Cardell?" Mr. Garland was asking. "Are we partners?"

He extended his hand, and after only a moment's hesitation, Damaris took it.

Partners.

Chapter Two

The hackney drove sedately down the long loop of road and stopped at the imposing iron gates. The gatekeeper peered at the well-dressed gentleman and the genteel lady in the carriage, tugged at his forelock, and hastened to open.

Ambrose Garland crossed legs encased in faultless breeches and well-fitting boots, flicked a speck of lint from his immaculate cuffs, and leaned back to smile at his companion. "Well, dear 'sister,' " he observed, "we are at Pardom."

Damaris clasped her hands tightly in the lap of her worn but still serviceable pelisse. "It seems that we are."

"It's a fine property," Garland approved. "Good farmland—wheat and rye mainly, and sheep in the hills."

No wonder, Damaris mused, that the earl had thought nothing of offering Desmond Winter four hundred pounds for a mere book. For the past half hour they had been passing through countryside dotted with red and white cows, sheep, orchards, and valleys crisscrossed with trout brooks—all of which belonged to my lord of Pardom.

"He's said to be one of the warmest men in England," Garland said as they passed a paddock filled with mettlesome horses and a riding track next to imposing stables. "A pity the man has no son. His daughter will inherit a great deal, but the title will go to a nephew when the present earl dies."

Damaris accepted this information as a matter of course. Since deciding to take the earl's offer, she and Garland had systematically split forces. While Damaris had written a letter to Pardom requesting permission to bring along "my sister and secretary, Miss Damaris Winter," Garland had set out to research the earl, his heir, and his property. He had also read all of Damaris's books so as to be able to carry out his masquerade.

Like a good general, Damaris had repressed her own reservations and assured her family that the earl was sure to be satisfied with the latest Lord Tedell book. "I shall call it *The Heir of Brandon Manor*," she announced. "The Earl of Brandon will be Pardom's fictional alter ego. And since he has long wanted a son, he should be glad to have a fictional one."

Damaris's brothers and sisters had been suitably impressed, but Lord Cardell, who considered this a caper-witted scheme, had looked worried.

The dowager had snapped, "I cannot like any of this. That a daughter of Sir Everard Cardell should have to resort to trickery—not that we are not grateful to you, my dear Ambrose—is the outside of enough. I trust that you will not live to regret this, Damaris."

Damaris hoped not, too. In spite of her outward calm, she had not been able to sleep for the past several nights, and when they boarded the mail coach at Maidstone early this morning, she had felt almost physically ill. In fact, when they had arrived at the Sussex town of Carling several hours later, she had had to fight a hen-hearted desire to run away.

Without Mr. Garland, she would never have come this far. It was he who had taken charge in Carling, insisting that she refresh herself with a luncheon at the local inn. His easy address and savoir faire had impressed even Mrs. Freddstick, the Junoesque landlady of the Silver Snail, and Damaris told herself that he would just as easily manage the earl. But try as she would, she could not be easy.

She felt her tension mount now as their hackney slowed before an imposing stone manor. From Garland's research, she knew that it had been built in the fifteenth century and that Henry VIII and his bride Catherine Howard had once deigned to stay and hunt at Pardom. Even now the place had an air of noblesse oblige about it, and Damaris watched uneasily as two junior footmen materialized to set down the hackney's steps.

Garland alighted first and helped Damaris down. "*Bon courage*, as the Frogs say," he murmured.

She admired his cool blood. Her own heart was beating hard as she took his proffered arm and ascended the flight of stone steps that led to the house.

A dignified footman greeted them at the great oaken door. Garland negligently handed the man a card, whereupon another and even more regal personage appeared, announced that he was named Murton, and begged Mr. and Miss Winter to step up to the study on the second floor.

As they ascended a handsome circular stair, Damaris looked about her cautiously. Although everything attested to Pardom's great wealth, she had the sense that something was lacking in this house. It was only when they had been ushered into a large room opposite the landing that she realized what it was. Pardom Hall was uncompromisingly masculine. There was no softening female touches anywhere.

As for the earl's study, it had the look of some old and exclusive gentlemen's club. There was a great deal of comfortable leather furniture, hunt scenes on the wall, and somewhat dusty occasional tables cluttered with snuff jars, pipes, newspaper clippings heavily underlined in ink, copies of the *Gentleman's Magazine*, whips and fishing flies, and a bowl of apples. On one leather armchair reposed an open book.

"*Lord Tedell's Revenge*—by Desmond Winter, of course," Garland said. He smiled encouragingly at Damaris and added, "This is not going to be difficult after all."

Damaris looked doubtful.

"The earl is obviously a man who likes his old, comfortable things about him," Garland continued. "I had an uncle like that once. Eccentric, was Uncle Brian, but a nice old fellow. Pardom's probably cut from the same cloth. Lots of bark, but not much bite."

He strolled over to admire an enormous silver bowl that was filled with trout flies, empty cans of tobacco, a battered hunting hat, an advertisement touting a boxing match to be held in Carling, several racing forms ripped in two, and diamond-stud cuff links set in gold.

"Most definitely eccentric," he murmured.

Damaris was looking about her. "I wish I could agree with you," she said unhappily, "but I am persuaded that the earl is not as you paint him. I do not think he is pleasant, and I would say that he can bite as well as bark."

"Really?" Garland picked up the cuff links and weighed them in his hand.

"Yes. I would say that Pardom is more than a little self-centered. I collect that he may be a difficult employer, someone who hates to be wrong. I fear he is also what Papa used to refer to as a 'stiff-rumped curmudgeon.' "

"A very accurate assessment."

The new voice came from behind her. Garland dropped the cuff links he had been holding. Damaris whipped around so quickly that the hem of her skirt caught a box of fishing flies and upended them on the floor. As they scattered everywhere, she stared at the tall man who stood framed in the doorway. But, she thought disjointedly, Pardom should have been an older man.

The personage in the doorway could not be more than thirty. He carried his six feet and more in an erect stance, had dark hair cut unfashionably short, and eyes the color of an early dawn sky.

"How did you arrive at those remarkable conclusions?" he was asking.

Before Damaris could form a reply, Garland made his bow. "I beg to introduce myself—I am Desmond Winter, and this is my sister, Miss Winter. Am I addressing the Earl of Pardom?"

The tall man's light gray eyes flicked to Garland. "No," he said.

He turned back to Damaris and continued, "Tell me how you come to know so much about the earl."

"I do not *know*, really," Damaris faltered. "I was merely guessing from what I could see in this room."

The tall man looked about the disheveled study and crossed his arms across his broad chest. "Yes?" he prompted.

"The floor is carefully swept and polished," Damaris began reluctantly, "but the tables are not dusted. I collect that this is because the maids do not dare disturb the earl's things."

"I see. But why do you think he will not admit to being wrong?"

"The newspaper clippings have several passages underlined in ink. They are all conservative views, and I suspect that they are the earl's views, also. A man who takes such a narrow view is apt to accept no opinion except his own." Damaris paused to draw breath. "And . . . and then there are racing forms which have been torn in two. I take it that the horses the earl backed did not place. Since he is rich enough not to worry about losing money, his anger must have come at backing the wrong horse."

Garland had been listening to Damaris in horror. He hastened to say, "Of course, sir, none of this is fact. My sister enjoys flights of fancy."

He was ignored. "And selfish?" the gray-eyed man inquired. "Why do you think Pardom is selfish?"

Damaris looked at Garland in mute despair. He drew a forefinger across his throat. "I—I saw that everywhere in this house there are signs of the earl. Everything is masculine. I found no hint that a young lady is in residence—no arrangements of flowers, no softening watercolors, no needlework sampler. And I did not say, 'selfish,' sir. I said, 'self-centered.' "

"You have a good eye, ma'am—and a clever mind." Unexpectedly the tall man smiled. Damaris was surprised that the humorous glint in his eyes made him look quite friendly.

Somewhat reassured by that unlooked-for warmth but still wary, she protested, "My brother is right. I am being fanciful, sir. I had researched just such a personage for *A Lady of Mystery*, and—"

"My sister," Garland interposed, "does much of the research for my books."

"How fortunate you are." The gray-eyed man inclined his head in a slight bow. "I'm Nicholas Sinclair."

This was the earl's nephew, the heir to the title. Having learned from Mr. Garland's research that Lord Sinclair was a rich man in his own right, a hero of the Napoleonic wars, and definitely no fool, Damaris's wariness increased.

"The earl's ridden to Carling," his lordship was saying, "but you'll meet him at dinner. I hope you'll be comfortable at Pardom. Is there anything you particularly need in order to begin your work?"

"You are very kind, my lord. We require only a room in which to write."

As the writer spoke, Lord Sinclair took his measure. Winter was no simpering mushroom but an extremely handsome fellow with an athletic physique. His smile was frank and open, he had direct blue eyes, and he carried himself well.

Sinclair owned himself pleasantly surprised in Winter's sister-secretary, too. He had expected a rabbit-toothed female with mincing ways, and instead here was a dark-eyed woman with an intriguing sense of observation.

Damaris Winter had drawn his uncle to the life, and now she was appraising *him*. For the first time in many months, Sinclair owned himself amused and intrigued.

"Murton will see you situated. Is there anything else you require?" he asked.

Garland looked at Damaris, who said, "Will I—will *we* have permission to walk about the property? I collect that the earl wished to have the book set here in Pardom, so we must be familiar with the grounds and the house."

When she turned her head, sunlight caught out the lights in her extraordinary hair. Sinclair could not decide whether it was auburn or red, or black like her eyes.

"Of course," he said aloud.

"Capital," Winter said heartily. "You are very kind, my lord. Very obliging indeed."

Lord Sinclair nodded, said they would meet again at dinner, and walked out of the room. Garland exhaled loudly and rolled his eyes at his supposed sister.

"Thank God that's over. I thought we were dished up."

Damaris was watching the door through which his lordship had exited. "We may yet be," she murmured.

"Nonsense. You have the nephew's approval. Now all we need to do is win over the uncle."

Damaris, who was not in the least sanguine about Lord Sinclair's approval, said nothing. She remained silent as the dignified Murton entered the study and informed the supposed Winters that perhaps they would consider the Blue Room a suitable workroom. "And your chambers have also been readied," he added. "These servants will see to your needs and do whatever you may require."

Garland nonchalantly followed the manservant who would act as his valet, but Damaris inwardly winced at Murton's delicate reference to the fact that they had not brought their own servants with them. She was silent as she followed her own escort, a stout and vivacious young Yorkshirewoman called Nancy, to a room on the third floor.

Like the rest of the house, this room bore no sign of feminine imprint. It was a large room with heavy period furniture, rich, dark hangings, and a large, square bed. On the walls hung more hunt scenes and a lithograph of the Romans battling the Gauls.

"I wonder where the earl's daughter is," she mused aloud.

"Lady Liza is with Miss Fuffletter, ma'am," her

abigail replied cheerfully. "Taking her lessons this time of day. It's the master's orders."

Damaris conjured up a picture of a pale, slender girl bending over her books. No doubt a tyrant like Pardom would have a meek and servile daughter.

"Poor child," she could not help saying. "I hope I shall meet her soon."

Nancy gave her a merry look. "Nay, tha will an' all. Now, ma'am, I'll unpack, shall I? It will make tha feel more at home."

The small word lodged like a quiver in Damaris's heart. She thought of home—of Hetty teaching the twins their lessons, of little Belle's chatter, of Peter chopping wood, and Grandpapa working on his wondrous machine.

I must get to work at once, Damaris thought. As soon as she finished *The Heir of Brandon Manor*, she could forget her masquerade and go home.

After she had unpacked, Damaris requested Nancy to lead her to the Blue Room, a square chamber with blue wallpaper, somber blue draperies, and a cobalt blue carpet that was scarred with cigar burns. Amongst the heavy furniture was a Jacobean writing desk.

"Tha'll do champion here, ma'am," Nancy said. "It's so quiet that tha can hear a mouse sneeze. I'll get the paper and pens, now, shall I?"

When her abigail had gone, Damaris went to the window and opened it. Outside, a tall chestnut tree grew so close to the house that its branches almost seemed to press against the panes. She could hear a robin chirping amongst the leaves, and sunlight changed the yellowing leaves to gold. A scent of woodsmoke, leaves, and grass wafted up to her on a lazy spiral of smoke.

"Come," she murmured, "this is more like it."

As she turned away from the window, she heard

a giggle behind her. Then, suddenly, there was a scrabbling, scraping sound and the sharp crack of a branch breaking. "Oh, devil fly off," a clear young voice exclaimed.

Damaris stifled a shriek as someone catapulted through the open window and fell into the room. Next moment she was staring at a young, fair-haired woman who was seated on the floor.

"Oh, *devil* fly off," the young woman repeated, "I have torn my dress."

"Who are you?" Damaris gasped.

"Lizabeth Beekley, but don't call me that." The young woman got to her feet and tried to straighten her unflattering dress of faded blue muslin. "I hate the name. I imagine Papa was dipping rather deep when he chose it."

"Aha," Damaris said. The image of the earl's frail, downtrodden daughter had vanished like April snow. "Well, Lady Lizabeth—"

"Don't call me that, neither," her ladyship commanded. "And 'Beekley' makes me think of a sour old crow like that Fuffletter female. Call me Liza." She paused and added with an endearing eagerness, "You're Miss Winter, ain't you? Now, that's a capital name. Makes you think of winter shooting and skating."

Frank hazel eyes, as clear as a woodland lake, smiled up at Damaris out of a piquant, heart-shaped face. "Miss Winter will not do," she exclaimed. "Pray call me Damaris."

Liza grinned and held out her hand. It was, Damaris noted, a pretty, slender hand, but covered with scratches and even a callus. "Then we are all right and tight," she declared. "I like you. If you had been like my latest governess, I should have been ready to scream. I often wish that Papa will fly into a passion and dismiss her as he dismissed the others."

She started toward the window again. "Why are you going down by way of the tree?" Damaris asked, curious.

"Because I like to climb trees. Besides," the earl's daughter added, "it will horrify Fuffletter when she finds out. She wants me to sit by the window and twiddle my thumbs over some curst embroidery hoop. Climbing trees is much more fun."

It was the same sort of thing that Peter would have said. Damaris returned Liza's grin and said, "Beware of dead branches, then."

The earl's daughter went to the window, swung her leg over the sill, and slid out onto the tree. Damaris watched somewhat apprehensively, but Liza was a skillful climber and descended swiftly. She had almost reached the ground when a horrified shriek rent the air.

"Oh, my dear Lady Lizabeth!" a shrill voice exclaimed. "What are you doing in that tree?"

Distracted, Liza looked down, and her foot slipped on the branch. Damaris uttered a cry of distress as the girl lost her handhold and fell to the ground. There was a sickening thud and then silence.

"Liza," Damaris shouted, "Liza, are you hurt?"

For answer, there was another earsplitting shriek. Damaris picked up her skirts and ran out of the room and down two flights of stairs. Then she was out of a side door and skimming around the house until the great chestnut tree came into view. Kneeling on the grass was a middle-aged woman in a green dress. She was shaking the supine Liza and imploring her to open her eyes.

"Do not tell me that you are dead," she wailed. "Oh, what will the earl say?"

"I beg you will not shake her in that way," Damaris cried, distressed. "She may have injured her spine or her head and should not be moved."

Pale green eyes, edged with colorless lashes,

peered up, and Damaris looked down into a long, narrow face equipped with a high-bridged nose, almost nonexistent chin, and a small mouth now tight with apprehension.

"I am not responsible," she twittered. "Lady Lizabeth climbed the tree of her own free will."

"Is someone hurt here?"

Ambrose Garland had come around the bend of the house and was walking toward them. "I heard a scream," he continued. "Good Lord—did she faint?"

Just then Liza opened her eyes and stared confusedly about her. "Devil fly off," she muttered. "Did I fall out of that tree, Damaris? That was a sapskulled thing to do."

Damaris knelt down beside her. "Can you move your arms and legs, Liza? And when you look at me, do you see one or two?"

"Only one. *And* only one of Miss Fuffletter, I'm glad to say."

"Oh, my lamb, my angel, you have returned to us." The lady in green had clasped her hands to her narrow chest and was swaying back and forth. "Ask, only ask, what I have suffered when I saw you fall. Ask if I were not ready to rend my hair from grief."

But Liza had suddenly become aware of Garland standing nearby. "Oh," she exclaimed. "Who are you, sir?"

"Desmond Winter, at your service, ma'am." Smiling, Garland got down on one knee and captured Liza's hand in his. "Behold me at your feet."

Liza had never seen such blue eyes before, nor hair that was the color of rich, ripe wheat. And Mr. Winter had the most wondrous voice. She stared at him, tongue-tied, as Damaris said, "This is Lady Lizabeth, Desmond. She has just had a bad fall and must not be overexcited."

"No, no," Miss Fuffletter chimed in, "she must rest. Oh, I pray that the earl does not hear of this!"

"Hey, what's this? What am I supposed not to hear?"

Miss Fuffletter gave a little shriek as a large, florid man stalked through the garden toward them. He was dressed in riding clothes and carried a crop tucked under one arm. Disapproving, protuberant eyes were fixed on the girl on the ground.

"What have you done this time?" he growled. Then, turning to the governess, he snapped, "What happened here?"

Miss Fuffletter seemed to shrink back into herself turtle-wise. "It is nothing—a mere accident," she stammered. "You need not be disturbed, sir."

"I fell out of that tree," Liza said shortly.

The earl glowered even harder, and Damaris regarded Pardom with intense dislike. The earl, she decided, was every bit as unpleasant as she had imagined.

"Oh," Miss Fuffletter was moaning, "Do not go further, do not reproach me, my lord earl. As one who is cousin to Lady Cordelia Armstother of Worcester, I know my duty. It is my fault that your daughter defied your orders and climbed yon tree. I have been negligent. I have been counted and found wanting. Alas, I should bear your displeasure."

She all but groveled on the ground. In a somewhat mollified tone the earl grumbled, "I told the chit I wouldn't stand for her starts. Mean to be obeyed. Shut her up in her room till tomorrow without her dinner."

Liza shrugged defiantly. Miss Fuffletter groaned out further abasement. Damaris felt compelled to protest, "But that would be unwise, sir. Your daughter has suffered a bad fall and should be watched for signs of concussion."

Irascible, red-rimmed eyes swiveled toward her. "And who the hell are you?" the earl wanted to know.

"It's Miss Winter, Papa," Liza said, adding loyally, "She's a right 'un, too."

Miss Fufflетter rolled her pale eyes heavenward. "I implore you, my love," she moaned, "do not use cant. It is not meet or fitting to a young lady, but more for a harum-scarum boy—"

"Oh, stubble it, will you?" growled the earl. "Females—they make more noise than a roomful of cats. So you're Desmond Winter's sister?"

Damaris curtsied, silently, but the earl's attention had already shifted. "Then you must be Winter. Wanted to be here to meet you," continued the earl. "Would have been back from Carling earlier if it wasn't for Arabella Neece."

"So that's why your goose is pissed." Liza calmly got to her feet and dusted herself off. "Miss Neece," she explained to Damaris, "lives a few miles east of Pardom. She's a great gun, but she ain't happy unless she's got a Cause. Right now she's trying to shut down a gaming house in Carling. Did Miss Neece hand you a jaw-me-dead after she caught you gaming at Siddons's, Papa?"

The earl shot a black look at his daughter. "What business is it of yours?" he demanded angrily.

Garland thought it time he cast oil on troubled waters. "I've been most anxious to meet you, my lord earl," he said. "I've wanted to discuss the plot of *The Heir of Brandon Manor* with you."

Pardom was immediately diverted. "That the title, is it? *The Heir of Brandon Manor.* Not bad. Got a certain ring to it."

"I am glad of that, sir," Garland said earnestly. "I think you will also approve of the character of the Earl of Brandon. It goes without saying that I hope to get your advice in all things."

His voice was sincere without being effusive. It conveyed admiration but not humility. The earl's choleric countenance softened.

"Got sense in your cockloft," he approved. "Always take good advice, my boy. *I* take my nephew's advice. He's a downy one, Nicholas."

"And a hero as well," Garland pointed out smoothly. "Lord Sinclair was decorated for valor at Corunna and again at Waterloo, was he not? He's almost as brave a soldier as yourself, sir, if that is possible."

The earl's wattles turned crimson with pleasure. "I served my country in my salad days—a few years only—neither here or there. Didn't think anyone remembered."

Garland smiled respectfully. This was going better than he had hoped, and he would have pursued the topic had not Lord Sinclair joined the party at this point. The nephew was another sort of bird entirely and demanded different treatment.

As Sinclair returned Garland's dignified bow, he was thinking that he might have been wrong about Desmond Winter. The man spoke, acted, and dressed like a gentleman, after all—

Then he glanced at the writer's sister. Damaris Winter had discarded her traveling cloak and was wearing a dress of amber muslin. Though it was newly trimmed and worn with a certain dash, Sinclair's knowledgeable eye could tell that the dress was not in its first youth. The waistline was not up under the bosom as in the new styles, but instead delineated Miss Winter's slender waist. Moreover, he discerned a neatly mended tear near the hem.

Again, Sinclair found himself intrigued. Why, he wondered, did the brother dress like a gentleman of fashion and let his sister look like a poor relation? Of course, one was the writer and the other merely his secretary, and he had met doting females before this, women who gave all their love and devotion to their male relatives. But judging from what little demonstration he had had of Miss Damaris Winter's wit, he did not think her the type of female who would be contented with the crumbs from her brother's table.

Damaris realized that Lord Sinclair was watching her. Unaccountably disconcerted by his appraisal, she turned to Liza and said, "I am persuaded that you should lie down. If you like, I will go with you."

Miss Fuffletter bridled at this. "No, indeed. It is I who will share *dear* Lady Lizabeth's disgrace. I am sure that my cousin, Lady Cordelia, has taught me how to do my duty. As to Lady Lizabeth, she has no doubt learned a lesson from this sorry day—"

"I have," Liza interrupted cooly. "From now on I'll be careful when and where I climb a tree. There's a lot of unsound branches in the chestnut, Papa. You'd best trim it."

"I'll trim *you*." But Damaris noted that the earl was grinning. He reached out and lightly cuffed Liza's cheek with what was almost affection. "Be off with you. Now, Winter, a word with you about your book."

As Pardom turned away, Damaris was struck by the eager look Liza sent after him.

Of course, she thought.

Pardom wanted a son. Liza wanted her father's approval. As Grandpapa would say, it was only scientific that Liza therefore climb trees, use cant, and swear. Even her air of nonchalance was a sham—

There was a rasping sound nearby as Miss Fuffletter cleared her throat. "Come, my love," the governess twittered. "No, Miss Winter, do not trouble yourself, I beg."

Once more Damaris was aware that Lord Sinclair was looking at her. Perhaps it was merely her writer's imagination, but she thought she saw suspicion in those light gray eyes.

Damaris promised herself that in future she would avoid his lordship as much as possible. After all, Liza was not the only fraud at Pardom.

Chapter Three

Pausing on the second-floor landing, Damaris looked yearningly out of the window. Early morning rains had given way to a glorious September afternoon with blue skies and fleecy white clouds, and a linnet was singing out its heart in the topiary hedge. She wished that she could be outside walking in the garden, but Lord Tedell's adventures held her prisoner.

She had just gone to her room to fetch the notes she had scribbled last night and was now on her way back to work. Meanwhile, beneath the window, the earl and Ambrose Garland were walking. Pardom was gesturing broadly, and Mr. Garland was nodding. They seemed in perfect charity, and Damaris was grateful. "Desmond Winter" had thoroughly charmed the earl.

But her pleasure dimmed as the earl clutched his chest and began to stagger about. "Bother!" she exclaimed.

"What's that?"

Lord Sinclair was coming up the stairs. He was

wearing his riding clothes, and his lean cheeks were ruddy with exercise. He looked to be the picture of health and vitality, Damaris thought, except for the listless look in his eyes.

He came to stand beside her on the wide landing and looked down at the scene below. "I see," he said dryly. "My uncle has had yet another idea for the book."

Damaris sighed. "This is the fifth time we have had to change the plot."

"Why doesn't your brother tell him that you can't work this way? Pardom will drive you mad if you let him."

Damaris had long ago come to this conclusion. She had also consulted with Ambrose Garland on finding a diplomatic way of asking the earl to leave them alone. Quoting Garland now, she said, "The earl is our patron. His wishes must be given every consideration."

Sinclair noted the worried frown that puckered Miss Damaris Winter's white forehead. The sun was shining directly on her and threw the too sharp bones of her face in hard relief. She was too thin, Sinclair thought, and there was a decidedly tense look in her black eyes.

What made Winter smile so easily while his sister acted as though the cares of the world were piled upon her slender shoulders? And while Winter's hands were spotless and well manicured, Damaris's fingers were stained with ink. There was even a smudge of ink on her small nose.

A ripple of interest stirred through the ennui that had clung to Sinclair all morning. "How's the book coming?" he asked.

"Beginnings are difficult," Damaris replied. She did not want to admit that she had not progressed past the first chapter of the commissioned book.

"Lord Tedell has arrived at Brandon Manor, and met the Earl of Brandon and his son, Cedric."

"No murders yet? No blood and gore?"

"Before characters are murdered, they have to be introduced," she pointed out.

Sinclair was amused at her matter-of-fact tone. He noted that the sunlight caused her hair to glow like burning coal and was wondering whether it would feel cool or warm to the touch when Damaris exclaimed, "There is your cousin, sir. I collect that she has returned from riding."

With some difficulty Sinclair shifted his attention to the garden, where Liza had joined her father and Winter. She wore a riding habit that was cut as close to breeches as was decently possible, and her hands were thrust into her pockets. On her head perched a disreputable cap that had belonged to one of the grooms.

"She must have escaped her governess again," Sinclair commented. "I don't envy the woman her task—Liza can be a harum-scarum brat who enjoys riding to hounds more than she likes her lessons."

"I cannot say I blame her. Edward and Peter and I would often play truant on a beautiful day and take the horses for a canter through the northern downs. Sometimes Hetty would join us, too."

"Are these people also your siblings?"

His question brought Damaris up short. "They are my—my cousins," she said hastily. "We are very close. That is, Peter and Hetty and I are. Edward is—Edward was killed at Waterloo."

She saw his eyes narrow and belatedly recalled that Lord Sinclair had also fought at Waterloo. "I am sorry, my lord," she said contritely. "I did not mean to bring back painful memories."

But he shook his head. "Nonsense, Miss Winter. It all happened a long time ago. My sympathies for your cousin."

He went past her up the stairs, leaving Damaris feeling depressed. Not only had talk of Edward opened unhealed wounds, but her usually fertile mind still did not want to work.

Perhaps that was because she was not used to being cooped indoors for such long periods of time. Back at Cardell House, after all, there had been all her regular chores to do as well as the writing. Damaris wistfully looked down at the garden. Perhaps, if she allowed herself a *small* walk outside, inspiration would come?

Acting before she could reconsider, Damaris ran down the stairs and opened a side door. She had hardly stepped outside when she heard Pardom roar, "Why does that woman need to meddle? Tell me that."

Somewhat alarmed, Damaris looked about her but could see no one. "I tell you," the earl's loud voice continued to complain, "Arabella Neece has gone too far this time. Embarrassed me in front of my friends. Asked me why I was such a gull-catcher as to play at Siddons's. No skin off her nose if I play piquet or faro or macao once in a while, is it? Ain't asking *her* to pay my vowels, curse it."

There was a soothing murmur, and Damaris could see the top of Ambrose Garland's fair head over a nearby topiary hedge. "No business of Arabella's if Siddons has a gaming house above his eatery," the earl growled. "*She* says that unsavory characters frequent the place, that the cards are fuzzed. She *says* that there are ivory tuners at work. Says that the law should intervene. Curst nonsense, all of it, but she's got the town stirred up."

As she listened, Damaris felt the beginnings of inspiration stir in her brain. "Gaming," she murmured. "Of course."

The writer's block that had held her captive had finally loosened its hold. Cedric, the fictional heir of Brandon Manor, was going to be a gamester. He was going to lose his fortune at cards, and thus would meet the villain, Sir Cuthbert Hackensell, who would lead him into the worst kind of gaming hells—

Damaris's flight of fancy stopped in its tracks. She had no idea what a gaming hell looked like.

This was a problem. Her Lord Tedell novels had been painstakingly researched, and she had never before described any scene without knowledge of it. "Supposing I go to Carling and see this eating house for myself?" Damaris mused. "Nancy will know how to get to town."

Nancy was more than glad to assist her mistress. "Research for the book, is it? There's nowt easier, ma'am. All tha needs do is call for the barouche and tell the driver to take tha to Carling. About an hour's drive, it is. Will Mr. Winter be going also?"

But he was still with the earl, and now that she had discovered her direction with the book, Damaris did not want to wait. Surely there would be no harm in going to Carling alone in broad daylight, she reasoned. After all, she needed no more than a good look at the outside of Ben Siddons's eating house and would be back long before dinner.

Ten minutes found her on the road to Carling. As she was driven toward the town, Damaris tried to fix her plan for Lord Tedell's latest adventure in her mind, but try as she would, the plot still would not fall cleanly into place. So engrossed was she in her thoughts that she hardly realized that they had reached Carling until the barouche rattled past the Silver Snail.

"Can you take me to Siddons's establishment?" she asked the driver.

The man looked surprised but urged the horses forward over the cobbled main street. As they went along, Damaris noted that some kind of disturbance was going on. She could hear shouts interspersed by the blare of a huntsman's horn.

"What is that noise?" she wondered.

The driver shook his head. "It's coming from Siddons's, miss," he said doubtfully. "Will you be wanting to change direction?"

Damaris instructed him to drive on, but this soon proved impossible. A large crowd had congregated in this section of the town, and the blast of the horn was deafening. Damaris signaled the driver to stop. "I will get out here," she told the man. "Please to wait for me at the Silver Snail."

The crowd was so dense that she had to push her way through, and it took some time before Damaris arrived at an open space. Here a dozen women—Damaris recognized the large landlady of the Silver Snail amongst them—were ranged about a tall lady with a coronet of iron gray hair and a lean, handsome, high-cheekboned face. This lady was carrying a horn, which she blew at regular intervals.

"Den of iniquity!" called this lady in a rich contralto. *Ta-ra* went the horn. "Anglers in the lake of darkness!" *Ta-ra!* "What? Siddons's gamin' house is givin' the town a bad smell, and we want it closed."

Damaris noted that several of the spectators were in agreement with this. Others were vocally opposed and expostulating that it was no business of Miss Neece's.

"I am an honest man making an honest living," one man was shouting in a high, nasal voice. "Mine is a perfectly respectable establishment, Miss Neece."

"Ha!" responded the tall lady. "I like that. What? How many sapskulls have you fleeced upstairs, eh, Siddons? How many sheep-brained idiots have you driven to desperation? To say nothin' of the unsavory characters that have started hangin' around

Carling since you began your little venture. Thieves and murderers, I shouldn't wonder. Flies go to manure, after all."

By standing on her tiptoes, Damaris could see an ornate restaurant behind Miss Neece and her followers. At the door of the eatery stood a rotund individual in a curly beaver. He was dressed in the kick of fashion in a maroon jacket with brass buttons, a shirt with a collar that rose up to his cheeks, and high-waisted pantaloons that tightly encased his heavy flanks. He was looking daggers at Miss Neece.

"That is slander," he called. "You would be wise to retreat, madam, before I call upon the law to dislodge you."

As if on cue, several official-looking individuals came marching upon the scene. One of them was a tall, fat man with a sweep of mustache. He looked worriedly at the gray-haired lady and sucked hard at his mustache.

"See 'ere, modom," he began. "You're victimizing a respectable citizen and creating a disturbance in the town. You'll 'ave to stop."

Miss Neece pointed her hunting horn at him. "There you are at last, constable," she exclaimed. "Arrest that card-fuzzin', dice-loadin' ivory tuner, Siddons. He and the moneylenders that run tame in his gamin' hell have ruined many lives, and now they're ruinin' Carling."

It was as though a light had flashed in Damaris's brain. With the force of a thunderclap, she realized what her plot would be. After taking Cedric to the gaming hell and ruining him, the foul Sir Cuthbert would introduce the heir of Brandon Manor to a moneylender. Shortly thereafter, the moneylender would be found murdered, and Cedric would be blamed.

"The moneylender will be found lying on his

hearth with a dagger in his heart," Damaris mused. "Or perhaps I should have him shot."

Miss Neece was shouting, "Arrest me, is it, you pie-faced prawn? What? I'll *give* you arrest!"

She and the other women advanced on the constable, who gave way. With the attention of the entire crowd focused on Miss Neece, Damaris saw her chance. Amidst the shouts, threats, and counterthreats that followed, she slipped through the crowd and walked into Ben Siddons's restaurant.

No one paid any attention to her. Siddons and his various employees as well as the scant handful of diners were all watching the events in the street. Hastily reconnoitering, Damaris noted a staircase at the other end of the restaurant. She approached it cautiously and saw that the staircase led to a landing and a door.

She had no doubt that behind that door lay the gaming hell she had come to research. And as though to confirm Damaris's suspicion, the door opened and a heavily muscled individual in footman's livery came hulking out.

He hooked a finger at one of the waiters and croaked, "What's the lay? The coves upstairs is getting restless."

Damaris, who had slipped into concealing shadows behind the staircase, saw the waiter shrug. "That old vulture, Miss Neece, is being arrested."

"You're not slumguzzling me?" When assured that this was not the case, the doorman descended the stairs, saying gleefully, "I got to clap me glims on that wunnerful sight."

Damaris shrank back even farther into the shadows. Then, when both men had passed her on the way to the outer door, she drew a bracing breath. It was now or never. Without thought of the consequence, Damaris whipped up the stairs.

At the closed door, she paused to look over her

shoulder. So far, no one had noticed her. Carefully turning the doorknob, Damaris whisked through the door and closed it behind her.

One could have expected that a gambling hell would be painted in sulfurous colors and that an aura of wickedness should emanate from it. Instead, this establishment was merely thick with cigar smoke.

Vaguely disappointed, Damaris slid behind a convenient pile of chairs that had been upended in a corner and looked about her at a room that was large and well appointed with portraits in costly frames, statuary, mirrors, and fine crystal. The drawn window hangings were made of gold velvet, and the luxurious carpet underfoot was obviously expensive. Waiters carrying decanters of brandy and various potations were circulating amongst the tables that had been set about the room.

At these tables sat the gamesters. Perhaps because of the commotion outside, there were few players, but these few seemed totally intent on playing faro, macao, or other games of chance.

Damaris noted that most of the players looked to be gently born. She let her gaze rove about the room until it settled on one fair young man who could have been the unfortunate Cedric of her novel. Apparently the fair-haired boy was in bad straits, for Damaris observed that he was perspiring heavily, and that his long white hands were shaking. At intervals he would throw down his cards and groan—then sign a piece of paper that was thrust in front of him.

The doorman had resumed his post and was periodically opening the door to new clients. Other players took their departures. Through all this coming and going, the fair-haired young man kept playing and losing. Finally one of the men at his table tossed down his cards. "That's all for today," he said. "Go home, Widdersby."

The young fellow rose to his feet and pushed back his chair with such violence that it fell to the floor. "No, you don't!" Damaris heard him exclaim. "I want to play. What's the matter? You've got my vowels, ain't you?"

"You're at point-non-plus," replied the other coldly. "Your IOUs are no longer any good. If you want to join the game again, you'll need some blunt."

The man called Widdersby swore loudly. "The pater will see me in hell before he gives me any money." His voice fell, and he began to plead. "You're a friend of mine, ain't you? One more game, and I'll make good my losses."

Damaris felt a wave of almost unbearable pity. She held her breath as the other man shook his head. "Go home, you young fool," he said.

His voice was hard. Just such a voice would Sir Cuthbert use on the unfortunate Cedric. Damaris felt desperately sorry for Widdersby, especially as she could hear him muttering under his breath.

"I'll get it," he was saying. "I'll go to a cent-per-cent. I'll show you."

Just then the doorman admitted a new group of clients. There were six of them, and Damaris was instantly aware of a difference between the newcomers and the other patrons. Five of them were dressed in workmen's clothes, and one man, apparently their leader, affected a bright blue coat, green corduroy pantaloons, and a canary yellow waistcoat embroidered with flowers. His thick, dark hair shone with oil, his smile glinted with a gold tooth. Though he was attempting to pass himself off as a gentleman, both he and his retainers looked thoroughly unsavory.

Damaris listened with keen interest as Blue Coat

asked what the lay was outside. "Never clapped me ogles on so many rozzers in all me puff," he exclaimed. "And all to arrest a bunch o' morts led by one old 'arridan."

"You wouldn't say that if you knew 'er," growled the doorkeeper. "That's Miss Neece. Father was a lord. She means to get this place closed down."

Blue Coat shook his head sadly. "Females," he said. "Enough to give a man 'ives."

He broke off as the fair-haired Widdersby stumbled against him. "Now, then, young sir," he murmured, "you're looking pale. Are you needing assistance? Sit down, 'ere, that's the barber."

Damaris could not hear Widdersby's reply, but Blue Coat put a beringed hand on his shoulder and turned him in the direction of a table very close to where Damaris was hiding. They began to talk in low tones until Blue Coat drew out a paper and placed it before Widdersby. The young man hesitated no more than a moment before signing it.

"Well done, young sir," said Blue Coat, pocketing the paper and drawing a clinking bag from his pocket. "Now, there's many as will fork you or slumguzzle you in this business, but Barnaby White won't whiddle you." He paused, and his face became menacing. "But if you was to 'op the twig on us—"

So this was a moneylender. A— what was the term? a "cent-per-cent." No wonder he had had to bribe the doorman in order to gain admittance here. Torn between horror and fascination, Damaris watched Widdersby go back to his gaming. She wished that Barnaby White and his cohorts would move away from her hiding place, but there seemed little likelihood of this. Damaris's heart sank as a passing waiter placed glasses of brandy on the table.

"Go easy, Mole," White cautioned. "You know what we're 'ere for."

"Aye, Barnaby," one of his unprepossessing followers growled. "But what if 'e don't come?"

"Does a fish swim? Of course 'e'll come."

His coarse voice sickened Damaris. She had seen and heard more than enough and would have gladly left the place, but unfortunately, there was no way to do so without being seen by the doorman.

Not knowing what else to do, she remained hidden and watched as table after table emptied and were filled again by men playing piquet and hazard. Her knees and arms became numb and her back ached, but the writer in her was fascinated by the various ways in which men lost their fortunes. Some strode out in anger. Others looked bored or despairing or nonchalantly tossed their IOUs—their "vowels"—on the table. Meanwhile White and his ruffians sat and drank and kept watching the door.

Her legs had cramped up so badly that she could hardly move them. Damaris realized that soon she *would* have to stretch her limbs or risk being frozen forever in her present position. She had just sent up a fervent prayer that something—anything—would distract attention long enough for her to make her escape when the door opened again, and a gentleman walked in. Damaris started as she recognized Ambrose Garland.

Here was rescue! In her thankfulness at seeing him, she did not even wonder how he had known she would be there. She attempted to signal him without giving away her hiding place, but she had grown stiff and clumsy. When she tried to move, her elbow caught one of the stacked chairs and sent it crashing against the others.

Garland swung about on his heel, stared at Damaris kneeling on the ground, and exclaimed, "Good God!" The players at the tables, White and his henchmen—everyone stared, and the doorman growled, " 'Ere then, 'ere, what's this?"

Striding over to Damaris, Garland grasped her by the arms and hauled her to her feet. "Are you hurt?" he demanded sharply.

She shook her head and looked hopefully at the door, but there was no getting around the big bruiser who was coming toward them. Ambrose Garland apparently had the same thought, for he rapped out, "No use trying to evade the law, madam. Thought you could create a disturbance in town and get away, did you? You'll join your friends in lockup." To the advancing doorman he added, "These women are the devil. This is one of Miss Neece's followers that nearly got away."

Winking at the doorman, he propelled Damaris out the door. "What were you doing in there?" he demanded.

"Research." Damaris was in such a hurry to be gone that she tripped on her skirt and nearly tumbled down the stairs into a staring waiter's arms.

Garland caught her by the arm. "Careful," he admonished. "You don't want to break your neck. *What* research?"

"For the book, of course. I needed to know what a gaming hell was like because Cedric is going to gamble away his inheritance and fall into the clutches of Sir Cuthbert."

They had exited from the restaurant as she spoke, and Damaris noted that while she had been inside, the sun had set. The nearly deserted streets made the town look secretive and even sinister.

"Why didn't you simply ask me what a gaming hall looked like?" Garland asked.

Damaris rubbed her sore joints as she confessed, "Actually, I have always wanted to do my research by myself—it is so much easier to write about something one has seen for oneself—but Grandmama would not permit it. And I thought—I thought it would not bother me, but there was so much unhappiness in there. One poor young man lost all he owned and had to borrow from moneylenders."

As she spoke, Damaris heard a sound behind them. Turning her head, she saw that Barnaby White's men had come out of the eatery and were looking up and down the street. With a muffled oath, Garland hustled her into the shadows of a side alley. "Be still," he hissed.

"But why should they wish to hurt us?" Damaris argued. "We have done nothing to them."

"*There* they are!"

At Barnaby White's shout, Damaris's heart seemed to leap into her throat. Her heart had commenced to hammer, and she wanted to do nothing more than run away. But when Garland snapped, "Run for it—I'll try to hold them off," she knew she could not be so cowardly as to leave the man who had come to her rescue to face the ruffians alone.

Looking about her wildly, she saw that someone had left an umbrella propped up against the alley wall. She snatched it up and shouted, "Help! Help!"

The word was knocked almost back into her lungs as one of the ruffians lunged at her. She lashed out at him with all her force, and the umbrella caught him across the face. Snarling and cursing, he fell back.

"Help," Damaris screamed again. "Fire!"

Rough hands seized her. A hand covered her mouth. "Shut yer muzzle," a voice snarled, "or you'll be sorry you was ever born."

Suddenly the ruffian was hurled aside, and a tall, dark-haired man stood in his place. "Get behind me," Lord Sinclair ordered.

He struck out with his walking stick, and one of the ruffians fell, half-stunned, to the ground. " 'Oo arsked yer to interfere?" snarled the raffish leader.

He strode forward, and Damaris saw faint light flicker on steel.

"Be careful," she warned. "He has a knife."

Next moment, the leader was staggering back with his hands clapped to his face. "You broke me bleedin' nose," he howled.

Sinclair advanced threateningly upon him, and the man ran. His followers hobbled after him, dragging their unconscious comrade with them.

"What are you doing here, Miss Winter?" Sinclair was beginning when he was interrupted by shouts in the near distance. Moments later a brigade of waiters, tradesmen, and constables, all of them carrying buckets of water, came running by.

"Where's the fire?" one of them roared. "What's ablaze?"

They rushed off in the direction that White and his henchmen had taken, and Damaris said, "Lord Tedell used that trick in *A Lady of Mystery*. When faced by twenty villains, he roused the town by shouting 'fire.' "

"It's an effective trick," Ambrose Garland approved. He had come to stand beside them and was brushing the dust from his coat. "See how the fools run."

"This is no laughing matter," Sinclair said sternly. "Your sister could have been hurt."

Garland sobered at once. "I know it. Damaris, I suspected something was amiss when your abigail said you'd gone to town. I know your passion for research sometimes lands you in trouble."

"Perhaps you care to explain?" Lord Sinclair drawled.

He had saved her from harm and she was grateful to him, so Damaris ignored his lordship's tone of voice. "I needed to discover what a gaming establishment was like," she began.

She broke off as Lord Sinclair's face became hard

with amazement. "You went into the *gaming house*?"

"Yes, but purely in the line of research," Damaris said. Since Lord Sinclair still looked scandalized, she pointed out, "The earl said that he enjoyed going to Siddons's. Have you never gamed there?"

It was on the tip of Sinclair's tongue to explain that he'd come to redeem a vowel for his uncle, who had not wanted to run the risk of meeting Arabella Neece while doing so. In the nick of time he reminded himself that he owed Miss Winter no explanations.

Coldly he said, "That's entirely a different matter."

"I do not see why it should be," Damaris retorted. "If a gentleman may go to a place such as that for sport, why should not a female? Although," she added as an afterthought, "I would never wish to. I cannot understand why gentlemen will throw their money away there and be forced to resort to going to a moneylender—a cent-per-cent, I believe it is called."

Sinclair was speechless.

"My sister can be headstrong," Garland interposed hastily. "Her excessive zeal in helping me sometimes leads her into the briars. I hope that it won't be necessary to tell the earl what has happened."

Even more coldly, his lordship said that he was not in the habit of carrying tales. "However, I suggest that Miss Winter refrain from such excessive zeal in the future."

Damaris had begun to resent the way the gentlemen were discussing her as if she were not even present. She did not care for Mr. Garland's fibs, and she misliked the way Lord Sinclair was looking down his aristocratic nose.

"I will keep that under consideration," she said coldly, and added even more frostily, "my lord."

Sinclair noted that Miss Damaris Winter's black eyes were snapping fire and that her small nose was tilted at a combative angle. No other female of his acquaintance would have dared to brave a gaming den by herself, and when he thought of her shouting "fire" to foil the ruffians and attacking her enemy with an umbrella—

Unexpectedly Sinclair wanted to laugh. He could feel a great wave of merriment welling up inside him, but managed at the last minute to turn it into a cough. After all, he did not want to encourage the unorthodox Miss Winter in her folly.

"I'm returning to Pardom Hall," he announced. "It may be wise if you follow suit—unless some other *research* keeps you here."

He touched his hat and strolled away, swinging his cane. Ambrose Garland watched him go with an odd look in his eyes. "That was a near thing," he muttered.

All at once Damaris thought of Barnaby White and his ruffians. She thought of what they might have done to her had not Lord Sinclair intervened. Irritation at his lordship's high-handed manner ebbed before the memory of White's knife.

Garland saw her grow pale. Reassuringly he threaded an arm through hers. "Nothing happened, thank heavens. But we must be more careful in the future, dear 'sister.' We must both be much more careful."

Chapter Four

"'A knowledge of the art of pugilism can never be acquired by theory alone,'" Damaris read aloud.

She put down *The Art of Boxing*, by Daniel Mendoza, and looked gloomily out the window. The fine September weather had turned sullen, and the skies were full of heavy clouds. And, to make matters worse, Lord Tedell had landed her in the soup again.

Damaris rubbed her aching forehead, thereby transferring a smear of ink to her temple.

Ever since her excursion to Carling, she had been hard at work on *The Heir of Brandon Manor*. Each day she had risen at dawn and repaired to the Blue Room, where, under her swift pen, the plot continued to take shape. Cedric had spent his fortune in gaming hells at the instigation of the crafty Sir Cuthbert, had all but broken his poor father's heart, and had borrowed heavily from a moneylender. Now that moneylender had been found with a bullet in him.

Of course, Lord Tedell did not believe for a moment that Cedric had killed anyone. In order to keep close watch on Sir Cuthbert, he set out to befriend the man. At this moment, Lord Tedell was accompanying Sir Cuthbert to a prizefight.

Unfortunately, Damaris knew nothing about prizefights.

The book Damaris had found in the earl's library told her how to parry an adversary's right with a left and how always to keep one's stomach guarded, but it did not give her a description of a pugilistic conflict or the atmosphere surrounding such an event.

Damaris rose from her chair, went to stand in front of a mirror that hung on the wall of the Blue Room, and pretended to punch with her right hand. Then she attempted a parry with her left.

"Whatever are you doing?" Liza giggled from the doorway. "Instead of drawing someone's claret, why not come for a drive?"

Damaris raised her eyebrows. "In this weather?"

"Mr. Winter and I are driving into the village." Liza smoothed her high-waisted vertical walking dress of lavender muslin. It should have been charming, but the color did not suit her, and the cut was bad. "There's a fine old Norman church he desires to observe for the book."

Damaris had not heard of the Norman church and had not planned to use it in the book, but no doubt its inclusion was another one of the earl's whims. She stifled a sigh and said, "That sounds most agreeable. I hope that it does not rain."

"That is what the Fuffletter says. She don't want to play chaperon, but of course, she's got to—unless you'll come, Damaris?" Liza asked hopefully.

Damaris gestured to the manuscript on the desk. "I wish I could. Still, I will walk with you to the door. I must return this book to the library."

On her way back to the Blue Room, Damaris met

Nancy, who exclaimed in her brisk way, "It's mithered tha looks, ma'am. Is there summat I can do for you?"

Damaris smiled wryly. "Not unless you have been to a prizefight, Nancy."

To her surprise, the abigail grinned. "Dunnot tell me that tha has the fight fever, too. All the gentle men belowstairs is talking about today's match."

Quite happily she settled down to gossip. According to Nancy, there was to be a prizefight in Carling that very afternoon. "Even Mr. Murton has brass riding on that there Fanworth, and my uncle Hector that lives in the village and my cousins are going theirselves to see the match." Nancy's grin widened. "Grandma is going as well. She's a great one for prizefights, my grandam, especially for a grudge match."

Damaris begged her to explain what a grudge match was, and Nancy explained that Fanworth, who was a local man, had been insulted by a Scotsman, George McCary. "Spit on Fanworth's boots, did McCary," Nancy explained with relish. "Called him a coward in front of his lass, which no flesh an' blood can fight, sithee. So now they're set to fight."

An idea had been formulating in Damaris's mind. "I would like above all things to go to Carling and see the match," she said. "Perhaps your uncle would be kind enough to take me with him and your cousins and grandmother?"

Nancy's eyes grew as round as saucers. "*Tha* go to a prizefight, ma'am?" she gasped. "It's not a fit place for a female, any road, let alone a lady like you. How would it *look*?"

"Your grandmother will be there," Damaris pointed out. "It will be quite proper. Come, Nancy, this is all research for my brother's book."

Looking dubious, Nancy said that she could put the matter to her uncle, and Damaris went back to the Blue Room to wait. Half an hour later the abigail bounced in to announce that her uncle was below and would be pleased to convey Miss Winter anywhere she wished.

"But," the abigail added with some asperity, "tha canst not go like that, ma'am. 'Twouldn't do, any road, to have a fine leddy like thysen ride to the fight along o' my uncle Hector and his family."

"I shall go disguised," Damaris agreed. "Do you have an old cloak I might borrow, Nancy? And a bonnet that will cover my face?"

Nancy produced a rusty black wool coat and the ugliest bonnet that Damaris had ever seen. "Begging tha pardon, ma'am, but anyone seeing tha now would think tha were a between maid," Nancy sighed. "I hope tha sees no one tha knows." Shaking her head, she led Damaris to the back door to meet her uncle.

Uncle Hector was a stout, broad-shouldered man with a bushy black beard. He wore a rusty black suit with a sprig of pinks in the lapel and owned a horse-drawn cart in need of springs. Mrs. Gregory was a silent, wizened lady who smelled of camphor, and Matt and Joe Gregory were round-eyed teenagers, so intimidated by the presence of a lady that they were tongue-tied for the entire hour it took to reach Carling.

They left it to Uncle Hector to entertain their guest, and Damaris found his talk fascinating. He apparently knew a great deal about prizefights, and as they drove toward the town, he instructed her on rules and technique, told her that no fighter might hit a downed adversary or seize him below the waist, and added that a man on his knees was considered down.

As they approached Carling, the traffic increased steadily, and by the time they had reached the outskirts of the town, the road was jammed with every kind of vehicle imaginable. There were gigs, post chaises, carriages, and curricles. As Uncle Hector's cart inched by the Silver Snail, Damaris noted that this establishment was crammed to the point of bursting with travelers.

"There'll be no room at the inn t'night," Uncle Hector prophesied. "But if tha thinks it crowded now, Miss Winter, tha should see how 'twas for an *important* match like the fight between Harry Lee and that Mendoza back in 1806. Lee was thirty-four and Mendoza older nor him, but that was a *fight*. It took fifty-three rounds for Mendoza to beat Lee."

The prizefight was to be held in an empty field near the inn. Damaris looked about her with interest and saw that in spite of what Nancy had said, there were several countrywomen present at this grudge match. The gentry was there as well. Damaris could see a number of curricles pulled by spanking grays and showy chestnuts, carriages driven by well-dressed individuals who ignored the rank and file who surged around them.

Damaris felt a prickle of anticipation laced with excitement as Uncle Hector maneuvered his cart to a standstill and paid an urchin to watch the horse. Then, with Damaris and Mrs. Gregory walking between them, he and his sons joined a long line to pay the entry fee.

Damaris tried to pass him some money, but he waved it away. "Tha'rt Hector Gregory's guest," he said, and nothing would persuade him to accept payment.

A rough stage had been erected in the center of the roped-off area. A few wooden benches had been set around the stage, but these were already occupied and there was standing room only for a large proportion of the audience. Other spectators had climbed onto the tops of their vehicles or even on the roof of the inn.

As Damaris was looking about her and taking mental notes, there was a roar from the crowd. One of the fighters had appeared from the inn. The crowd parted for him to pass and roared again as he vaulted into the ring. "That's Fanworth," Uncle Hector whispered proudly. "Yon's our lad."

In a few moments, another man, smaller but more muscular and with long, hanging arms, leaped up onto the stage. He had a hard-bitten face and an insolent manner, and his appearance caused as many boos as cheers. "McCary," Uncle Hector said, unnecessarily.

Damaris watched with great interest as the seconds arrived and the combatants chose umpires from the crowd. "To decide all the disputes in the ring," Uncle Hector explained. The seconds then tossed for corners, and the two men stripped down to their breeches and faced each other.

Bare fists were raised. "They're coming up to scratch—time's been announced—and now they're at it," Uncle Hector breathed. "Mix it oop, now. Mix it oop!"

At first the men simply parried each other's punches. Then McCary let loose with a lightning left jab. "Wilta let him catch thee napping?" roared Uncle Hector, outraged. "Go to it, lad, mix it oop, I tell thee."

Suddenly the opponents closed on each other. Until now, Damaris had been enjoying herself. Now, suddenly, she realized how brutal a prizefight could be. She felt sickened as the large Fanworth punched his opponent in the ribs, then smashed him in the face and in the belly.

"Right, lad," Uncle Hector bellowed. "Now tha's getting somewhere."

Uncle Hector and his sons had forgotten about Damaris. Everyone, including the women, was shouting and yelling. Suddenly McCary sprang forward and hit his opponent on the jaw. Fanworth staggered back, and a roar of distress swelled through the crowd. McCary hit again, but this time his blow did not connect. Fanworth dodged the blow but lost his footing in the process. He staggered back, slipped, and fell heavily.

There was a howl from the crowd, and old Grandma Gregory suddenly came to life and screamed like a banshee. "Foul! He warn't hit!" she screeched. "Get up, man, and go to the line or tha will be counted out!"

Fanworth lay where he had fallen. His legs twitched, but he could not get up. As time was counted and still Fanworth could not rise to go to the line, the shouting of the crowd rose to a crescendo. Many voices took up Mrs. Gregory's cry of "Foul!"

Damaris tugged at Uncle Hector's arm. "Mr. Gregory," she shouted, "is the fight over?"

Uncle Hector stopped in midyell, stared at Damaris, and apparently recollected that he had females in his care. "Our lad wasn't fairly downed by that McCary. 'Twas a foul. No one will want to pay oop their bets, and there's bound to be trouble." He waved a paw at the boys. "Let's get out of here, lads! We don't want harm to come to the women."

Together with his sons, he began to push his way through the suddenly churning, milling crowd of spectators. What had been a holiday crowd was now a press of hostile, angry people demanding their money back.

A crowd of fight-mad countrymen began a scuffle, and more joined in. Suddenly a drunken sot lurched between her and Uncle Hector, and then all hell broke loose. Damaris was swept up by a crowd that dragged her almost into the heart of the melee.

Pushed and pulled, she tried to stand her ground, but it was a losing battle. All around her, fights were erupting as spectators who had had too much to drink fought out their differences of opinion. Bettors were refusing to pay, and shouts and oaths turned the air blue.

Suddenly Damaris found her arm caught and held. She turned swiftly, but her relief was short-lived when she saw not Uncle Hector, but a young gentleman in a puce-colored coat with large brass buttons. With him were several other young bloods. "All alone, pretty?" the gentleman shouted. "Hold on then, and we'll get you out of it."

He and his companions began to battle their way through the crowd, laying about them with their canes and a bottle of brandy that one of them was carrying. Damaris tried but could not break free and was dragged along until they had come clear of the mob.

Here the young man who had rescued Damaris turned to her. "What a crush." He grinned. "Got the breath squeezed out of you, ain't you, little love?"

He followed this question with a squeeze of his own. Forgetting that she was dressed as a servant, Damaris snapped, "How dare you? Let me go at once!"

The young man laughed—yodeled was perhaps a better description—and drew her closer. "Not so fast, beauty," he said, exhaling a wave of brandy-soaked breath. "Where's my reward for risking my life to get you out of the crush, hey?"

"You are foxed," Damaris said indignantly. "If you do not unhand me, I will—"

"High in the instep for a tweeny, ain't you?" Then he yelped as Damaris kicked him squarely in the shins. He let her go and she turned swiftly on her heel and began to hasten away.

His inebriated companions all burst out laughing, and one of them sneered, "Can't even handle a cozy armful, Monty? Show you how to do it."

He caught Damaris by the waist and hauled her backward. She could not kick him, but she dug her elbows backward and heard an "Oof" as she contacted a soft stomach. Yet for all that, his grip only tightened.

"Hellcat!" He was laughing but then broke off to yelp in pain as she turned in his grip and aimed a stinging box at his ear. "Kick and claw, will you?" he added furiously. "You should be taught a lesson."

"A lesson needs to be taught, certainly," a familiar voice said.

The man holding Damaris captive gave a squawk of pain as a strong hand descended on his arm and almost dislocated his shoulder. "The lady said no," Lord Sinclair explained.

The young fop loosened his hold on Damaris, who pulled free. She looked thankfully up at Sinclair, but he was busy assessing the inebriated group of young bucks. Their blood was up, and brandy-courage was making them foolishly daring.

"Think of what you're doing," he said sharply. "You are in a public place and constables are nearby. Do you want to spend a night in the round-house for assaulting a serving wench? I thought not. Be off with you at once."

Angry but cowed by Lord Sinclair's air of command, the young men made themselves scarce. "Well, Miss Winter," his lordship then said, "we meet again."

Smarting at being called a serving wench, Damaris spoke stiffly. "And once again it seems that I must thank you."

He gave her an ironic bow. "First a gaming house and then a prizefight. I'll say one thing for you, Miss Winter. You are energetic."

Damaris bridled at his tone. Then the humor of the situation touched her and she laughed ruefully. "Perhaps 'energetic' is not the word for it."

When she smiled, her dark eyes danced, and her too thin face softened into something like beauty. In spite of himself, Sinclair returned her smile.

"Why are you dressed in servants' clothes?" he wondered.

"Nancy said that I should." Damaris looked about her in consternation. "Where is Mr. Gregory?"

Sinclair pointed out that since he had no idea who Mr. Gregory was, he could not be hoped to produce him. "He is Nancy's—that is, my abigail's—uncle. He very kindly allowed me to ride down to Carling in his cart with Matt and Joe and old Mrs. Gregory. I am sure," Damaris continued, ignoring the rising incredulity in Lord Sinclair's eyes, "that they are searching everywhere for me."

"Then we will wait until they arrive," Sinclair replied. He drew her out of the path of the spectators, who were now walking back to their vehicles. "I gather this is more research for the book?"

His tone was resigned, but when she glanced up at him, Damaris noted that his eyes were alight with amusement. This merriment wholly transformed his face. It was, Damaris thought, as though the sun had suddenly burst through dark clouds.

"And no doubt your brother is searching for you along with this Mr. Gregory and Joe and Matt," Lord Sinclair continued.

"He does not know that I have come here. And," Damaris added hastily, "I am glad I came, though I would never want to see another prizefight. It is a brutal sport, but it has an atmosphere, a *feel*, that is indescribable. I hope I can capture it." She stopped short, realizing her slip, and amended, "I mean, I hope that my brother can capture it in words."

Sinclair looked surprised. "Hasn't he ever been to a prizefight? Most men have."

"Desmond is a sensitive man and does not care for such violence," Damaris explained.

But he was not sensitive enough to spare his sister such sights. Damaris read the unspoken thought in Lord Sinclair's suddenly dry expression. "My brother and I work together, my lord," she said stiffly. "I hope that you are not going to preach propriety to me."

"Not I, Madam Mystery."

Damaris looked up at him uncertainly, but he was not being disagreeable. His smile had returned, and he looked decidedly friendly.

"I am not overly fond of prizefights myself," he was saying. "I came out of curiosity. It's said that Fanworth may be as good a fighter as Gentleman Jackson ever was. It is a pity about today, but he will fight again and win."

As he spoke, Damaris heard a hail over the general noise. Uncle Hector and his sons, one of whom carried Mrs. Gregory on his broad back, came hurrying toward them.

"Eh, miss," the Yorkshireman cried, "There th'art—" He broke off and eyed Lord Sinclair speculatively.

"Lord Sinclair found me by accident," Damaris explained. "I am sorry that you were so anxious, Mr. Gregory. I am ready to return with you now."

But Uncle Hector shook his head at this. It were more fitting, he said, that Lord Sinclair should convey Miss Winter back to Pardom. "Th'art the earl's nephew and all, sir," he added as explanation. "I know tha'll take good care of the lady."

He bowed to Sinclair with such dignity that his lordship bowed back and gravely thanked him for his trust. Damaris also thanked Uncle Hector, who professed himself delighted that he had been of use to Miss Winter, and then went off to reclaim their cart and horse.

Damaris watched them go. "Mr. Gregory," she declared, "is a true gentleman."

Sinclair liked her for the sincerity in her voice. Most ladies would have turned their noses up at a rough-spoken man with plain ways, but Damaris Winter was no ordinary woman. He was glad that he had decided to stop to see the prizefight, and even more so that he had found her when he did. When he thought of those young fools frightening her, he felt a rush of anger. Then he recalled how effectively she had defended herself, and the smile returned to his eyes.

"We should return to Pardom before you think of anything else to research," he said.

As if his words were some sort of signal, the heavens opened up. Rain did not fall—it sluiced down as though some celestial dam had been broken. Before Damaris could gather her wits together, Lord Sinclair caught her around the waist.

"What are you doing?" she cried.

"Getting under cover—unless you have a better plan?" He tossed his cloak over them both, and began to shove his way toward the Silver Snail.

The common room of the inn was crowded to the bursting point, the air thick with smoke and the noise deafening. Using his powerful shoulders, Sinclair pushed his way through until he had managed to win through to a tiny space in a corner of the room. Here he stood in front of Damaris, protecting her from the crush.

"Are you all right?" he asked.

"Yes, thank you."

But she felt unaccountably breathless. Lord Sinclair was standing so close to her that she could feel his warm breath on her cheek. Though he had removed his arm from around her waist, he was still standing very near to her in the crowded place, and she was acutely conscious of being pressed against his long, lean length. Above the stink of tobacco and brandy, she took in his lordship's clean, outdoors scent.

"It is—close in here," she managed.

Sinclair had been thinking the same thing. He had moreover realized that Damaris Winter's slenderness was deceptive. She was, he realized somewhat disjointedly, rounded in all the right places.

He attempted to clear his head by breathing deeply—a trick he had learned on the peninsula—and became conscious of a subtle flower fragrance that emanated from her. Roses . . . or violets, perhaps? wondered Sinclair, who had never learned to tell one flower from the other.

He cleared his throat twice before trusting himself to say, "I had hoped we could commandeer a private parlor, but that seems hopeless. At least we're dry in here. It's a sudden squall and will soon pass."

Damaris attempted a businesslike air. "Meanwhile," she said briskly, "this place is a wonderful source of atmosphere."

"More grist for the mill, Madam Mystery?"

Once more he had used the foolish nickname. She glanced up at him and saw that he was grinning so infectiously that she could not help smiling back. "The earl wants to include local color in the book, so I will— I mean that my *brother* will write about this inn," she said.

That was the second time she had made a slip of the tongue, and twice meant there was no coincidence. Sinclair was now sure that the girl did all the writing and that the brother took the credit.

"Coxcomb," he muttered under his breath.

Damaris did not hear him. A new wave of refugees had pushed themselves into the common room, and she found herself being crammed even closer to Lord Sinclair. Their bodies were pressed so immodestly close that even their knees were touching.

In an effort to think of something besides the proximity of his lordship, Damaris pretended to look about her. She noted that the large Mrs. Freddstick stood behind the tap, dispensing ale and conversation to her patrons. In this she was aided by a portly man who looked so much like her that they had to be related.

"Poor Mrs. Freddstick has her hands full," Damaris commented. "Did you know that she was one of the women who was arrested for trying to close the gaming hall? I am glad to see that she is out of prison."

"None of those women saw the inside of gaol," Sinclair said. "Arabella Neece has a great deal of influence and money."

"Miss Neece seems to be a strong-minded lady. Is it true that she always marches to a cause?"

"She marches to her own drummer, certainly. I've known Miss Neece since I was in leading strings, and I remember her to be one of the few people for whom my uncle Molyneux has a healthy respect. She can outshoot and outhunt him, and they have usually been in charity—except for this business of Siddons. Not that my uncle is a great gamester, but apparently Miss Neece abominates any kind of gambling."

Damaris thought of the young, fair-haired man she had seen at the gaming hall. "I am persuaded she is right," she said soberly. "*Has* Siddons's gambling hall been closed?"

"Due to the furor Miss Neece has caused, ugly rumors have begun to surface. It's said that Siddons is in league with moneylenders and that he loads the dice and fuzzes the cards. The townspeople want his establishment shut down, but Siddons has influence and money, too, so the matter is at a standstill." Lord Sinclair paused to add in a dry tone, "No one *forces* men to gamble. Like drinkers and liars, gamblers bring their troubles on themselves."

Damaris swallowed hard as she thought of the lies she had told since coming to Pardom. In a low voice she protested, "But people are not all bad or all good. There are many shades and shadows—and secrets, too—in people."

For a moment Sinclair let his own mind touch past darkness within him, the place of death and confusion and loss that he had sealed away and barred from conscious thought. It was for a moment only, and then he retreated from the carnage of Waterloo and the screams of his dying friends. Absently he raised his hand to rub the aching scar on his right arm.

"We are all human," Damaris was saying. "I am persuaded that if—"

She broke off suddenly, and he saw that she was staring at a group of men sitting in a corner. Sinclair was startled to recognize them as the ruffians who had been attacking the Winters near the gaming house.

"Do you know who those men are?" he asked sharply.

"I know that the one dressed in the yellow waistcoat is called Barnaby White," Damaris replied. "I believe he is a moneylender, for he lent money to that young man at the gaming hall."

As she spoke, White looked in their direction. His eyes met Damaris's squarely for a moment, and a speculative look gleamed in his eye. Then he saw the man with her, and he paled.

Muttering something to his henchmen, White got

to his feet. Then, together with his unprepossessing entourage, he shoved his way out of the crowded inn.

Possibly the man did not want a second hiding. Sinclair frowned. He had not liked the look White had given Damaris. It was almost as if the ruffian had sighted a quarry that had been eluding him.

"I wonder," Sinclair muttered.

If, as Damaris had said, every man had his secret, her brother could be no exception. Was it possible, Lord Sinclair asked himself, that Desmond Winter's secrets somehow involved Barnaby White?

Chapter Five

"Knew all the time that Sir Cuthbert was a villain," the Earl of Pardom said. "Tried to throw me off the scent, didn't you, Winter? Should've known you'd catch cold trying to gammon me."

He sat up in his well-worn leather armchair, prodded Garland jocosely with his riding crop, and chuckled. Garland put down the chapter from which he had been reading aloud and confessed that the earl was too quick for him.

"Thank God all my readers aren't as astute as you, sir," he said. "I'd never sell my books otherwise."

The earl's answering growl was actually a purr of satisfaction. Everything so far had been going famously. Winter would write, his sister would transcribe his notes. Now and then there would be a reading from the chapter in progress, which even Nicholas seemed to enjoy, and Pardom noted that *The Heir of Brandon Manor* was better than any of the other Lord Tedell books.

"Like how you describe me—*hem!*—that is to say,

how you describe the Earl of Brandon," the earl continued. "Fine fellow—every inch a gentleman. And Tedell's a wonder. Has a curst devious mind."

Lord Sinclair, who had been standing by the window and smoking a cigar, suggested, "Not as devious as the man who writes about him, perhaps."

Garland protested this. "That's doing it too brown, sir. In this case Lord Tedell is merely confusing Sir Cuthbert. To confuse the enemy is a lesson I learned during the war."

"Oh, were you in the war?" Sinclair wondered. "What regiment?"

"I meant that I had learned lessons in strategy *from* the war. We writers absorb all kinds of experiences in order to write about them."

The earl yawned. He felt sleepy and content, for lunch had been a hearty affair, and the port he had consumed with his cigar was making him feel quite mellow. "When d'you think the book will be finished?" he asked. "Not that I'm in a hurry, mind."

Sinclair felt a twinge of impatience. He was bored with his uncle's foolishness and would have gladly gone home except that he had the sense that he was still needed at Pardom. His instincts, which had kept him alive through the war, now told him that there was something about the writer that did not pass muster.

Could he be overreacting because Winter was taking shameful advantage of his sister? Being a cad, unfortunately, was no crime. Thoughtfully, Sinclair watched Winter get to his feet and stroll over to admire some silver candlesticks that reputedly had been the gift of Henry VIII.

There was a discreet knock, and Murton appeared to announce visitors. The earl took the card from the silver tray that his butler proffered and looked irritable and somewhat alarmed. "You ain't told her that I was in, Murton?"

A pained expression flickered through the butler's well-trained eyes. "I explained that you were not receiving visitors, m'lord, but Miss Neece suggested that I was mistaken and that she would wager her soul that you were smoking and drinking in your study."

"Curst female's come to rake me over the coals again for gaming at Siddons's," growled the earl. "Don't feel like seeing her. *You* go down, Nicholas, and tell her I ain't well."

Murton coughed discreetly behind his hand. "Miss Neece further intimated, m'lord, that if you were not feeling strong enough to come down to her, she would come up to you." He paused. "With her are Lady and Miss Freemont. I have shown them to the Green Saloon and have informed Lady Lizabeth of the ladies' arrival."

"Oh, why not?" growled the earl. "The more the merrier. You come down with me, Nicholas, don't rat on me. You too, Winter. You writers want to absorb experiences, don't you?"

With an air of profound gloom, he left his study and descended to the Green Saloon, where the three ladies waited. Pardom bowed stiffly, admitted to being their servant, and in the most ungracious tone welcomed them to his house.

"Though I don't know why you came out," he growled. "Going to rain soon, from the looks of it. Bound to catch a curst chill riding back home. Still . . . here you are. Nicholas, you recall Lady Freemont—neighbor of mine—and her daughter, don't you?"

"And he's sure to remember me," exclaimed the third lady in her impressive contralto. "What? You look a trifle hagged to me, Nicholas. Trottin' too hard, I shouldn't wonder."

She chuckled richly, causing Lady Freemont to look somewhat shocked. Though she had been Miss

Neece's neighbor for years, Lady Freemont could never quite get over that lady's outspoken ways. If she were not so well connected, Lady Freemont thought delicately, dear Arabella would be quite coarse.

"And who's that over there?" Miss Neece was inquiring. "Never tell me he's that writer you commandeered, Pardom. Writers are reedy, washed-out little squabs, ain't they? But this one's got a handsome phiz."

The earl preserved a lofty silence, but Miss Freemont giggled, which netted her a look of reproof from her mama.

"Indeed," Lady Freemont said in a languid voice, "it was to meet Mr. Winter that my daughter and I called today. As secretary of the Sussex Muses, Mr. Winter, I wish to welcome you to our midst. We are a small society but an earnest one, and we esteem the opportunity to meet a literary gentleman."

Expressing his pleasure, the supposed Desmond Winter bowed over Lady Freemont's hand. He then saluted Miss Freemont with a warmth that did not escape Sinclair's cynical gaze.

"Got another conquest, m'dear," Miss Neece laughed. "Don't bother with Caroline here, Winter. Half the countryside's danglin' after her."

"I can well believe it," Garland said. He sent Miss Freemont a speaking look as he added, "But even an unworthy soul may worship at the altar of the fair."

Miss Freemont blushed prettily. Lady Freemont looked complacent. "Spoken like a poet," Miss Neece exclaimed. "What? Ah, there you are, Liza."

Sinclair saw his cousin enter the room at this moment together with Damaris Winter. Neither of them looked happy to be there. Liza had a resentful expression on her face, and Miss Winter's eyes proclaimed her to be many miles away.

Actually Damaris was deep in the throes of her book, and Lord Tedell's problems were far more important to her than anything going on at Pardom. Since the day of the prizefight, she had virtually locked herself into the Blue Room and had left Mr. Garland to entertain the earl and Lord Sinclair.

Damaris was intensely aware that Lord Sinclair was standing by the many-paned windows. He was watching her, she knew. It was as much to avoid those keen eyes as to write that she had shut herself away.

She did not want to be in his company now, would not have been here if Liza had not knocked on the door and insisted that she come down to meet Miss Neece and the Freemonts. "You won't like them, mark my words," she had warned darkly, "but Miss Neece is a great gun."

There was no way Damaris could refuse. Besides, she was more than a little curious about Miss Neece, who, even without her hunting horn, was impressive. She was tall for a woman—almost as tall as the earl, Damaris judged—and in spite of her deep voice and abrupt, almost mannish speech, her sharp-boned features had a definite beauty. Her eyes were large, dark, and swimming with such intelligence and humor that Damaris liked her at once.

Mrs. Freemont was a bird of another feather. Dressed expensively in a dove gray silk day dress embroidered with roses, her ladyship was a stylishly faded beauty with a dissatisfied expression. After a languorous glance that took in Damaris's inky fingers and plain attire, she bowed rather coldly and turned away. Miss Freemont, meanwhile, proceeded to flutter her eyelashes at the handsome Mr. Winter.

Miss Freemont was fair, pretty, and dressed in exquisite taste. Damaris took careful note of the young lady's peach-colored flocked muslin dress with décolletage and puff sleeves, and her piquant bonnet trimmed with feathers and peach-colored roses, all the while thinking that she would dress Cedric's sweetheart, the Lady Hortensia, in such a costume.

Murton now entered together with servants carrying silver trays full of small cakes. "Might as well eat something now that you're here," the earl said grumpily. "What's that stuff, Murton? Ratafia—pah! Chuck the curst stuff out and bring something with teeth in it, man."

Lady Freemont looked pained and Miss Freemont archly protested that the earl sounded exactly like her papa. "But then, I collect that gentlemen have no taste for ratafia or lemonade."

She cast a sideways glance at Garland, who instantly said that he was very fond of lemonade. He insisted on serving Miss Freemont personally, and Sinclair observed this move with even more cynicism. Now, he thought, Winter would no doubt take a seat next to the Freemont girl.

Before he could do so, however, Liza strode across the room and plopped down beside Miss Freemont. "Can't I have some lemonade, too, Mr. Winter?" she demanded in a combative tone.

"Of course, ma'am. Lemonade for all the ladies." As Garland carried out this task, Sinclair left the window and strolled over to stand beside Damaris.

"You were not at today's reading," he remarked.

She shook her head. "I have been busy copying the latest chapter."

Idly he picked up her ink-stained hand and studied it. "How close are you to finishing the book?"

Damaris tried to extricate her hand, but Lord Sinclair was holding it fast. The warmth of his clasp reminded her of that evening in the Silver Snail. Even in that public place, she recalled, his lordship had managed to make her feel somehow vulnerable and compromised.

"I am not sure," she replied in what she hoped was a brisk tone, "but I *think* we are moving toward the crisis."

She had forgotten how warm his gray eyes could be when they glinted with humor. "How is your Lord Tedell going to trap Sir Cuthbert?" he asked.

"That is the stupidest thing I have ever heard!" Liza exclaimed.

The conversation died into shocked silence. Lord Sinclair dropped Damaris's hand, and Miss Freemont, who had been talking and laughing with the supposed Desmond Winter, stopped in midgiggle.

The earl scowled at his daughter and snapped, "What ails you now?"

"I am certain *I* do not know," Lady Freemont said in an offended tone. "I was merely suggesting that the style has changed again in London. Buried in the country, Lady Lizabeth could not know what dear Lady Jersey wore to the Duchess of Milfield's ball."

"I don't care about fashions," Liza mumbled, red-faced. "And I'm tired of talking about balls and people I don't even know."

Lady Freemont looked astounded at such rudeness. "Then what shall we talk about?" Miss Freemont wondered.

She fluttered her eyelashes at Garland, who remarked that perhaps Lady Lizabeth would rather choose the topic of conversation.

Liza flushed even more. She did not understand the emotions that raged through her whenever Mr. Winter looked at the lovely Miss Freemont. She sent a pleading look at Damaris, who hastily cast about for something to say.

"It—it has been a mild September," she began. "The harvests will no doubt be good this year."

"They will indeed if our tenant farmers work as they should," sniffed Lady Freemont. "I cannot but feel that the lower classes are the outside of enough. They *will* drink and gamble away all that they own."

Miss Neece raised her head sharply. "Speakin' of gamblin'," she said ominously, "We're still tryin' to rid Carling of that disgustin' gamin' den. What? The one you used to frequent, Pardom."

Affecting not to hear, the earl turned his back and stared out of the window.

"The lower classes are so trying, are they not?" Lady Freemont asked in her faint, well-bred voice. "Their thinking is quite incomprehensible. I understand that there was a vulgar prizefight in Carling, and even my groom—who has been in the family for years—went to see it and returned with a black eye and a swollen jaw. I would have dismissed him without a character, but Freemont said that we should give the man another chance." She turned to the supposed Desmond Winter. "But of course, sir, *you* are a poet and so cannot enjoy dreadful pursuits such as prizefights and gaming."

Garland's smile was ingenuous. "I confess I have once or twice sat down to cards. If that debases me in your eyes, ma'am, alas for me."

"No one would say such a thing," Lady Freemont said. "Gentlemen must have their diversions, after all."

"Ha," said Miss Neece in her rich voice, "that argument has become shopworn. What? If men have their diversions, what do we have? What's sauce for the gander should be sauce for the goose."

Pardom had slowly begun to turn crimson during this speech. Lady Freemont exclaimed, "I hope, dearest Arabella, that you are not about to tell me that men and women should be viewed as equals. Ladies have their sphere of influence, just as gentlemen do theirs. I, for one, would never gainsay the fact that men have dominance."

"Don't know about spheres," Miss Neece retorted. "What? Lot of chuckleheaded men around, though. *They* couldn't have dominance over an umbrella stand."

She and Pardom looked daggers at each other until the obviously horrified Lady Freemont engaged the earl in conversation. After a moment Miss Neece turned her attention to Damaris.

"I have been wonderin' where I saw you before," she said. "Now I know. You were the one who nipped past me and ran up the stairs to the gamblin' den."

Disarmed by the humor in the lady's eyes, Damaris relaxed into a rueful smile. "Was I so obvious?"

Miss Neece shook her head. "None of the others saw you. I suppose the gamin' hell was research for one of your books?"

"You have read my—my brother's books?" Damaris asked eagerly.

"Pardom lent them to me before we came to cuffs over the gamin' hall." Miss Neece drew a sharp breath that was almost a sigh. "Always have been tongue-valiant. What? Meant to make peace today when I came visitin'. Instead of which we're branglin' again."

She looked almost sadly at the earl and was silent for a moment. "Liked what I read of Desmond Winter's style," she then said. "Good action, mean to say. But I think Winter's wastin' his talents."

Damaris raised her eyebrows. "In what way?"

"Why don't Winter write somethin' with more depths? What? A book with a woman as the central character, for instance. Don't mean he should dish up one of those awful romances that Caroline Lamb puts out," Miss Neece explained judiciously, "but a good book. One that'll make you laugh and cry and think at the same time."

Damaris had thought of such a book before this. She had even suggested it to her publishers, but Dane and Palchard had informed her that a book with a female as the central character would not pay.

"It'd be interestin'," Miss Neece mused. "Think of it, Damaris—don't mind if I call you Damaris, what?—a female who'd be a woman of character and not some candy-box miss without two ideas in her head. She'd be brave enough to seize her chances, and of course, she'd have brains—"

Miss Neece was interrupted by a crash and an agonized wail from Miss Freemont, who jumped to her feet, clutching her skirts. "You did that on purpose," she shouted at Liza. "You spilled your horrid lemonade all over me!"

"My hand slipped—I'm sorry," Liza cried, but Miss Freemont was beside herself.

"How could you have been so clumsy?" she wailed. "You have ruined my dress."

"Devil fly off with your dress! I *told* you it was an accident!"

"Liza!" Sinclair said, sharply.

His cousin made a strangled sound, turned scarlet, and bolted from the room. Pardom seemed too astonished to move, but Sinclair and Damaris both followed Liza.

They met at the foot of the circular stairs.

"I am afraid that if you speak with her now, you will only upset her further," Damaris warned. "Pray let me try."

He frowned up the stairs. "What has got into the brat?"

Damaris thought of the day when Liza had

dressed in her best to drive into the village with the supposed Desmond Winter. "Liza is at an awkward age," she said carefully. "Even Hetty, who has the sweetest nature in the world, was all abroad at that time."

"Your cousin Hetty?" Sinclair asked, still frowning.

So absorbed had she been in Liza that she had forgotten who she was and to whom she talked. Recollecting herself with a jolt, Damaris stammered, "Yes, my—my cousin. Now I beg you will excuse me. I must go after Liza."

As she hurried up the stairs, she found that her heart had begun to pound. She had almost betrayed herself. "I had never thought it as hard to live a lie," she muttered under her breath.

She missed her family so much. There had been no word from Cardell House these last two weeks, and this worried her dreadfully. Sometimes at night she would wake up with a vague feeling of dread and wonder if Peter had succeeded in chopping off a leg or if Grandpapa had blown up the stable and himself with it. She would toss and turn and resolve to find some way to get word from Kent. But then, when dawn came, she would always convince herself to go on with the masquerade.

Damaris's thoughts broke off as Nancy came down the hall toward her. "Is Lady Liza in her room?" she asked.

"Aye, that she is, and that governess o' hers is with her." Nancy's usually vivacious face was troubled. "Begging tha pardon, ma'am, but is owt wrong? Miss Liza was crying without tears. Stonyfaced, like, as when her ma died."

Damaris blinked. "You mean she did not weep for her *mother*?"

"I wasn't in service then, but Mr. Murton says

that was how it was," Nancy replied. "He said that the earl would not allow tears."

"Oh, shame!" Damaris whispered.

"Nay, ma'am, it wasn't what tha thinks. Mr. Murton said that it wasn't that the earl was cruel-hearted but that he missed his countess so much. Sithee," Nancy pointed out, "I dunnot know this for a fact. But Mr. Murton once said that the countess was a gentle soul and that the earl loved her sore. When she died, happen he could not bear it."

Damaris was thoughtful as she knocked on Liza's door. There was no answer, so after knocking again, she opened the door and looked in. Liza was sitting on her bed and staring into space, and Miss Fufflетter was standing nearby and ineffectually wringing her hands.

She looked as Damaris entered the room and protested, "I do not think that this is the time to bother dear Lady Lizabeth."

"Shall I go away?" Damaris asked. Liza shook her head and Damaris continued, "Come, nothing can be so bad. If you are worried about Miss Freemont's dress, you need not. It will soon come clean."

"Oh, devil fly off with her and her dress," shouted Liza. She gulped hard and then burst out, "Did you see the way she was making sheep's eyes at him?"

"At *whom*, Lady Lizabeth?" demanded her shocked governess.

Ignoring Miss Fufflетter, Liza cried, "Damaris, he didn't even look at me. Caroline is so much p-p-prettier—"

Suddenly she exploded into tears. Damaris sat down on the bed, gathered the weeping girl into her arms, and rocked Liza as she had rocked all her brothers and sisters in their times of trouble. "Hush," she said, "it will come to rights. I promise you that it will come to rights."

"No, it never will," howled Liza. "I am as thin as a stick insect. I will never have a b-bosom."

Miss Fuffletter gasped. She put her hand on her own bony bosom and added, "A lady should never even *think* such things. If my cousin, Lady Cordelia, ever heard her daughters say such words, she would be beside herself. Besides which, you have a . . . a . . . front."

"Not like Miss Freemont's. I hate her, the cat! Did you *see* how the men toadeat her? And she has round hips," moaned Liza.

Miss Fuffletter made unintelligible croaking noises. "Oh, go away," Liza moaned. She buried her head in Damaris's shoulder and began to sob again. "I've made a perfect guy of myself and I wish I were dead."

The governess's narrow face quivered. She rose to her feet and stammered, "I can see that I am not wanted. I will leave you to Miss Winter. No doubt *she* can comfort you."

Damaris was truly sorry for Miss Fuffletter, but this was not the time to placate her, not with Liza crying so bitterly in her arms. She hushed the girl until her sobs lessened into an occasional sniffle. Then she said, "Now, that is all over. A good cry never hurt anyone, Liza. Indeed, my grandpapa tells me that it is good for a person, because all the impurities in the body are washed out with the tears."

"I must've had a lot of impurities." Liza laughed shakily, and Damaris knew that the crisis was over.

Since Liza flatly refused to return to the Green Saloon, Damaris went down and made excuses. Liza had the toothache, she said, and this made her irritable. The ladies agreed that the toothache was a terrible thing and rose to leave.

Miss Neece hung back apace. "Been meanin' to

talk to you about Liza," she informed the earl. "Have to say it's your fault, Molyneux."

Sarcastically the earl entreated Miss Neece to enlighten him, adding, "I suppose it's *my* fault that the chit is full of curst starts?"

"Yes it is," replied his companion. "If you'd paid proper attention to the gel after Clara died . . . But then, you was only thinkin' of yourself and your grief and not hers."

"Stubble it, Arabella—" Pardom rumbled, but Miss Neece would not allow him to continue.

"Tried to bully the poor little thing. What? Pretended not to care for her because she was a female. Wouldn't even admit to yourself you were fond of the child." She paused. "Were you frightened of gettin' too close to Liza, Molyneux? Afraid were you, that you might lose her as you lost Clara?"

The earl seemed past speech. He had turned magenta and was making incoherent sounds. Miss Neece turned her back on him and said clearly, "Nicholas, you tell Liza to visit me at Neece Place. What? Had my hands full with that Siddons business, but I've been thinkin' of her. And you come with her, Damaris. Got more ideas for that book we was talkin' of."

"What really ails Liza?" Lord Sinclair asked after Miss Neece had made her exit and the fuming earl had stamped out of the room.

"She is growing up."

Damaris did not care for the sudden, keen look Lord Sinclair bent on her. "Is the chit moonstruck over your brother?" he asked sharply.

His tone was intensely irritating, but Damaris kept her temper. "I think that you should talk to Liza—" she began, but he interrupted her.

"I'm asking *you*. Liza is barely seventeen. Any man who'd take advantage of a child in calf love—"

He broke off and added ominously, "I won't stand for any such foolishness."

"It is you who are being foolish!" With an effort, Damaris forced herself to speak more calmly. "My—my brother has taken advantage of nobody. And I warn you, sir, that to take that tone with Liza will not serve."

"I have known Liza somewhat longer than you have," he retorted.

For a moment, they glared at each other, and Damaris wondered how she could have thought for even one moment that Lord Sinclair could be in any way sympathetic. He was odious and high-handed and in his way, more horrid than his uncle.

Sinclair was meanwhile blaming himself for having allowed things to get to this point. He should have seen the signs that Liza was forming an unsuitable tendre for the writer fellow—*would* have seen it if it had not been for Damaris Winter. She had intrigued and interested him, had made him laugh. It was partly because of her he had been putting off a course of action that should have been implemented long ago.

Abruptly he said, "I am leaving for London early tomorrow. When I come back, I'll have a talk with Liza—and my uncle, too. That flutter-headed governess is doing my cousin no good. What Liza needs is some sort of a finishing school—something to put town brass into her."

What she *needed* was a father who cared for her, Damaris wanted to say, but she checked herself. She had remembered that she had no right to tell Lord Sinclair what to do.

But her expression must have betrayed her thoughts, for he spoke quite brusquely. "This is not one of your novels, Miss Winter. Do me the kindness of leaving my cousin alone."

Insufferable—odious—but, Damaris had to admit,

his lordship was also justified in his concern. It would not do to leave the impressionable Liza too long in the company of a handsome gentleman.

At least Mr. Garland *was* a gentleman and would realize the position they were in. Damaris was grateful when he himself brought it up that evening.

"This afternoon's contretemps was very embarrassing," Garland said. "Am I imagining it, or did Lady Lizabeth take exception to the fact that I was being polite to Miss Freemont?"

"She is at an impressionable age," Damaris said gently. "You have been kind to her, and she must have misinterpreted your attentions."

Garland pulled a rueful face. "Calf love can be painful," he agreed. "Have no fear—I'll do my best to quash this growing tendre in the bud. The last thing we want to do is to antagonize Nicholas Sinclair."

Lord Sinclair left for London early next morning, and Damaris spent the next day at her desk in the Blue Room. True to his promise, Garland stayed close to the earl and paid very little attention to Liza.

Damaris was still hard at work when Nancy brought up a letter for her. "This here came just this minute, ma'am," she said. "It were brought by an old gaffer that looks ready to pike away. Eh, but I forget the name—something that started with a B."

Damaris looked at the writing on the envelope and felt her heart contract with fear. "Bowens?" she whispered.

The letter was from Hetty. According to her, there had been a break-in at Cardell House and the burglar has taken all the spare cash there was. Hetty did not want to worry her sister, but there was no money left, and the butcher and the baker would not extend them any more credit. Was it, Harriet asked diffidently, possible to get an advance from Pardom?

"Where is the earl?" Damaris wondered, and Nancy said that he was shooting game in the north meadow.

Then she added shrewdly, "If you want summat from him, ma'am, happen you should send Mr. Winter to do the asking. The earl don't hold much with females, but he'll give your brother what he wants."

It was good advice. Damaris sought out Garland, who looked grave and agreed to go to Pardom at once.

"I must go home," Damaris fretted. "I will not be able to rest until I see how all of them are. Do you think you can possibly convince Pardom to let me go to Kent?"

Garland was gone a long time, but he brought back the promise of a hundred pounds.

"He wasn't pleased, but he agreed to let you have the advance," he reported. "I also persuaded him to allow you to deliver the money, but he absolutely refused to let me accompany you. The old buzzard wants me to dance attendance on him, more's the pity. Can you manage the trip alone?"

"Oh, yes—Bowens and I will take the mail coach. I truly thank you for all your good offices," Damaris added gratefully. "I will return as quickly as I can."

Damaris had known she had missed her family, but she had not realized how much until she saw the green-gold swell of the north downs against the sky. She could hardly contain her impatience as the mail coach deposited her and old Bowens at Maidstone, where Peter awaited them with the cart and Old Mope.

"I met every coach from Sussex," he confessed as he hugged his sister. He was so excited that his face was almost as red as his hair. "Such goings-on, Dami! We were woken up in the dead of night by a window smashing, and when we ran down, the house was in a shambles."

"Was anyone hurt?" Damaris gasped.

"No. Hepzibah squealed and said she was going to faint, but Grandmama said that if she fainted, she would be put on notice. She was a great gun, Dami—ordering the constables around like a general. You should have heard her."

"And Grandpapa?"

Peter's enthusiasm dimmed. "Grandpapa's locked himself in the stables. We're worried about him."

"Not the Wonder again?" Damaris groaned. "Never mind. You can tell me on the way home."

At Cardell House she was greeted eagerly by her siblings and by Hepzibah, who quavered, "Och, *ochon*, Miss Damaris, dear. What a turrible thing this is, to be sure. Each night, noo, I expect we'll be murdered in our beds."

The dowager Lady Cardell agreed. "This house is not safe, Damaris," she sniffed in an affronted tone. "What the world is coming to, I cannot tell you. In my day, an Englishman's home was his castle, and now it seems fair game for footpads, thatch-gallows, and thieves. I constantly implore your grandfather to employ a stout night watchman, but he never listens to *me*."

Damaris next went to see her grandfather, who was in the stable behind closed doors. When she shouted out that she had come home, he deigned to shoot two rusty bolts, give her admittance, and hug her even as he growled, "What're you home for? Told those fools not to bother you."

Damaris realized how thin her grandfather had become. His face had aged, and there were dark circles under his eyes. Even his hair had a drooping, dispirited look. "You are not well!" she exclaimed.

Lord Cardell ran a hand over the side of a huge metallic object at the side of the stables. "It's almost working, Damaris. 'Struth, it is. And when it goes—"

"We will all be rich and dress in silks and velvets and eat sugar and strawberries all day. That is all very well, but have *you* eaten your lunch today?"

"Who can eat the rubbish that Hepzibah cooks?" complained his lordship. Then he added somberly, "Don't mind telling you, Damaris—beside the bridge. Must make a push. 'Struth. Have to invent *something* that will bring us a honeyfall."

"Don't fear, Grandpapa." Damaris strove to sound cheerful. "The earl has given us an advance. A hundred pounds."

"And that is another thing," Lord Cardell continued. "I hate this deception. Queer stirrups indeed when a man has to stand by and let his granddaughter feed him through a lie."

A talk with Harriet worried Damaris further. According to Hetty, Lord Cardell had not eaten well nor slept since the robbery. "I did not want to write to you and alarm you, Dami, but I am most concerned," she sighed.

Damaris took a long look at her sister. Hetty and Liza were almost of an age, but there was a vast difference. Hetty was serious and had too much responsibility for her years, whereas Liza was still a pretty, empty-headed mayfly. Suddenly she wondered how Mr. Garland was striving to keep out of Liza's way.

The excitement of Damaris's return did not last long, and gloom returned to envelop the Cardells. Lady Cardell's sighs echoed through the house, Peter looked morose, and even Hetty could not get her younger siblings to smile. Belowstairs, Hepzibah chanted funereal dirges as she prepared the evening meal.

Damaris did eventually manage to coax Lord Cardell out of the stable to partake of this repast with his family, and under her watchful eye he ate a little. But there was no life and no light in him, and Damaris's worry became high anxiety when he refused to have a sip of the "medicinal" brandy that he hoarded.

Perhaps if she encouraged him to talk about his inventions? But even this brought no results. When pressed, Lord Cardell growled that he was now working on a trap for burglars. "Locking the barn after the damned horse has done a bolt," he added savagely.

They went to bed early, retiring promptly after dinner so as to conserve heat and candles. It was chilly in the house, and as Damaris snuggled into the bedclothes beside Hetty, her last waking thoughts were of the man who had burgled her family. She hoped that the knave *would* try again. She would dearly love to catch him at it.

On that vengeful thought she fell asleep and dreamed that she was walking in the garden at Pardom. A man came toward her, and she saw that it was Lord Sinclair. He doffed his hat to her and smiled, and then suddenly he changed to Mr. Garland, who was asking her if she would like to roll some dice with him. Then everyone was rolling dice, and that caused such a clatter—

She realized that Harriet was shaking her. "Dami," Harriet was crying. "Oh, Dami, wake up!"

The sound of the clattering dice became buzzers, bells, clangers, and noisemakers. Damaris leaped out of bed onto the cold floor. "What on earth is that racket?" she cried.

Snatching up her wrap, she ran downstairs. On

the stairs she met Peter and the twins. Lady Cardell, nightcap askew over long gray braids, appeared on the landing, and Lord Cardell hopped spryly down the stairs exclaiming, "We've got him. 'Struth! This time we've got the bugger."

The entire household followed. "Thought about it after we went to bed," Lord Cardell continued to babble. "Thought and thought . . . sometimes lightning *does* hit twice. Scientific thinking. So I set up my burglar traps all around the house. Just in case the varlet came back."

"It's more likely a passing rabbit," sniffed Lady Cardell, but Damaris noted she had a hatpin clutched in her hand.

She herself caught up the poker from the fireplace as she passed it. Peter had Edward's sword. Lord Cardell carried his stick. Hepzibah had a mop, which she swished about as she walked.

"Ready?" Lord Cardell demanded, and threw open the door.

Even in the darkness Damaris could discern that something was trapped in the net. It wriggled and squirmed and uttered muffled curses. "It *is* a burglar," Hepzibah shrieked. "Lord have mussy on us!"

"Ho, knave!" Stick raised, Lord Cardell approached the netted figure. "What've you got to say for yourself, miscreant?"

"That you had better get me out of this contraption at once," a familiar voice snapped.

Damaris almost fainted. They had not caught a burglar after all. They had caught Lord Sinclair.

Chapter Six

"Got him!"

Peter's triumphant whoop was a signal for general jubilation. The twins joined hands and danced around the captive in the net, Hepzibah brandished her mop, and the dowager ordered Bowens to run for the parish constable.

Amidst the confusion Damaris shouted, "Stop it! It is Lord Sinclair, the Earl of Pardom's nephew."

The awful silence that greeted this announcement was followed by a commotion of a different kind as Peter and the old gardener attempted to tug the net away from his lordship. The air was rent with bangs, clangs, whirs, buzzes, and Lord Cardell's entreaties that nobody damage his invention.

Throughout it all, Lord Sinclair preserved an ominous silence. Though it was far too dark to see his face, Damaris was certain he was enraged. But his anger was not her greatest problem.

She said, "My lord, I am very sorry for all this. We had been recently burgled, and my cousins were merely trying my granduncle Cardell's new burglar trap."

The twins stopped their shouting and turned to stare at their sister. In the excitement they had quite forgotten that Damaris was supposed to be "Miss Winter," but quick-witted Peter exclaimed, "Cousin Damaris is right, sir. You must think we're a regular ramshackle lot," and Harriet curtsied shyly and hoped that his lordship had not been hurt.

Sinclair was tired, hungry, and damp from the drizzle that had been falling for the past two hours. He had not anticipated one of his grays losing a shoe at Towbridge, nor had he expected to have a net fall over his head. He was about to impart a severe setdown when the dowager sniffed.

"Your appearance was unexpected, sir, to say the least," she declared coldly. "Ten o'clock is scarcely the time to make an unannounced visit."

Lamplight glinted on the business end of the hatpin she was holding, and suddenly Sinclair's sense of humor revived. He should have expected Damaris Winter's relatives to be an odd lot.

"My fault entirely, ma'am," he apologized. "I beg you'll pardon any inconvenience my, ah, unorthodox arrival has caused. I had not realized how late it was. Seeing the house in darkness, I was about to seek an inn when the heavens fell on me."

He bowed deeply and then turned to Lord Cardell. "At least, sir, you now know that your burglar trap works."

"Well said, young man!" The inventor skipped forward, hand outstretched. "Name's Cardell—welcome to my house. Quite an occasion, 'struth. Not every day you trap a lord."

Damaris watched as Lord Sinclair shook hands with her grandfather. Now that she had time to think, she remembered their last, less than cordial conversation.

"What are you doing here, my lord?" she asked somewhat warily.

Sinclair found himself at a loss. He could hardly explain that his business in London had heightened his suspicion of the Winters. He had become even more disquieted when he returned to Pardom and found Damaris gone, together with a hundred pounds of the earl's money.

Not for a moment believing Desmond Winter's explanation about a burglary in Kent, Sinclair had decided to come to Cardell House and see for himself what was going on. But, of course, he could not tell Damaris this.

He temporized, "When I returned from London, I learned about the burglary. My uncle was concerned for your safety and sent me after you. Apparently Lord Tedell can't finish his adventures without you."

He was interrupted by Lady Cardell, who desired to know why they were all standing outside in the wet. "You are welcome to the hospitality of Cardell House, my lord," she told Sinclair repressively, "even though this has been somewhat of a surprise."

Reminded of his duties as a host, Lord Cardell insisted that Lord Sinclair stay the night, dispatched old Bowens to the stable with his lordship's curricle, and desired Peter to give the gardener a hand. "And mind, be careful you don't knock anything over," he added. "Don't dare *touch* the Wonder."

"What is the Wonder?" Sinclair asked.

The old fellow clutched Sinclair's arm. "Work of my lifetime. It'll replace horses and make your curricle obsolete. Wave of the future, 'struth."

He laughed and nudged Lord Sinclair, who wondered if he had fallen into a nest of bedlamites. "I see," he said soothingly.

Lord Cardell continued to talk about his inventions as they progressed to the morning room, which, Damaris decided, was small and relatively comfortable besides being easy to heat. "Pray sit down, my lord," she said, "and we will stir up a fire and bring blankets and— Hepzibah, some tea, if you please. And brandy. Is there any brandy?"

There was a scant spoonful of the liquor in Lord Cardell's last bottle. "Saving it for my old age," his lordship sighed. "Don't regard me—hospitality is king. You'll need it, my boy, to hide the taste of the tea. I might," he added delicately, "have some myself. Not good to be out in the damp."

Lady Cardell announced loftily that she was going to retire, and swept the twins away in her wake. Meanwhile Peter brought in an armful of wood, and Hetty ran to spread sheets on the bed in the guest room, which, she and Damaris decided after a hasty conference, was the least drafty of the empty rooms and had no known leaks.

Sitting amidst this hum of activity, Sinclair felt an odd sense of contentment steal over him. The fire was warm, and the strange-tasting tea made bearable by the brandy, and besides, the Cardells were such a peculiar lot that they intrigued him.

To begin with, they were all redheaded. Miss Harriet had strawberry blond hair, the twins' curls were gingery, and Peter's shock of hair blazed like a sunset. Even the old fellow had a scattering of auburn hairs in his tufted eyebrows. The family resemblance was very strong, and Miss Winter and her pretty cousin Harriet, especially, looked almost like sisters.

Damaris noted his lordship's level gray gaze lingering on her and felt a quiver of apprehension. She did not believe for an instant that he had come after her simply because he was worried for her safety. He had some other reason, and whatever it was, she distrusted it.

"You were very kind to come so far to see to my safety," she said aloud, "but as you see, all is well. If you will tell my brother that I plan to return to Pardom in a day or two, I will be grateful."

His lordship hesitated, and Damaris prayed that he would agree to do as she asked. She cringed when her grandfather said expansively, "What, leave so soon? You must stay with us a few days, Sinclair. Might even let you see the Wonder."

"His lordship has affairs to attend to," Damaris interposed, adding meaningfully, "I am sure, my lord, that Lady Liza misses you."

Sinclair noted that Damaris's expressive black eyes were worried. She did not want him to stay, he thought.

"Liza is visiting Neece Place and doesn't even know I'm gone," he said. Then to Lord Cardell he added, "Does your nephew share your interest in science, sir?"

The old fellow looked blank, and Damaris was the one who answered, "You recall, Granduncle, that Desmond wrote about an inventor in *The House of Ravenmoor*."

"Of course I remember, Ain't in my dotage yet," Lord Cardell exclaimed tartly, but Sinclair had noted his hesitation.

"At any rate," Damaris was saying, "you would not enjoy staying at Cardell House. We are not at all what you are used to."

The more she protested, the more Sinclair was determined to accept Lord Cardell's invitation.

"Don't regard me," he said cheerfully. "I'm used to fending for myself and often travel light—as I have done tonight—without my valet or my groom."

He smiled at Lord Cardell. "And I'd enjoy learning more about . . . the Wonder."

After all, he reasoned, the longer he stayed with these Cardells, the more he would learn about Miss Winter and her brother.

Lord Cardell was flattered. He felt sure that Lord Sinclair was staying on because of an interest in science. Next morning early, Sinclair was awakened by a loud knock on his door, and the inventor's white head poking into his room.

"Thought you'd be up," he chirruped. "Best time now to get to the stables. 'Struth! Nobody to see us."

There seemed, Sinclair thought, no one about at all. The only servants he saw were the lugubrious-looking maid who brought up the water for Lord Sinclair's ablutions, and the old gardener who was pottering about in the kitchen garden.

Were there only two servants in the entire place? Sinclair wondered about this as he followed his host toward the stable. No doubt once a handsome property, Cardell House was in serious decline. The gardens were ragged and overgrown, the shrubbery in bad need of a pruning. The stable roof was sagging, and the walls wanted paint. The main house was holding up bravely, but it had two broken windowpanes on the north side, and several shingles had fallen down and were lying dejectedly amongst the rosebushes.

If Winter was such a successful writer, Sinclair asked himself, why did he not take care of his family? And why had he not come to Kent himself after the burglary?

There were so many questions about the man and precious few answers, Sinclair thought. He was deep in thought as they reached the stables, where

Lord Cardell hastened to insert a key in a rusty lock.

"In with you," he commanded. "Got to be quick—don't know who's hanging about trying to steal my ideas."

There were, Sinclair discovered, only three horses in the stable. These were his own matched grays and a swaybacked nag that was napping in its stall. Lord Cardell made soothing noises to the horses, then walked over to a large object that was covered with old blankets.

"Ready, young fellow?" He grinned and whipped off the covers.

Sinclair could think of nothing more to say than "Aha."

Lord Cardell's Wonder machine had once been a carriage. It still retained the wood-and-brass body and large wheels of such a conveyance, but was apparently propelled by steam rather than horses. It had a cylindrical boiler in the back and was steered by a single wheel in the front.

"You put the coal in here," the inventor said, tapping a trapdoor that had been cut into the boiler, "and it heats the water. The steam goes up these pipes here. Nothing new there, you'll say. Watt had his model steam carriage, you'll tell me. But," he added triumphantly, "Watt's contraption was too bulky for road use. Mine ain't."

Lord Cardell patted the flanks of his invention and crooned lovingly to it. "Answer's in my steam boiler. It's smaller, lighter, and more compact. Had some problems with pipes bursting in the past, but there's bound to be ups and downs in scientific progress. I've installed a foolproof system for the valves since. Want to see how it works, Sinclair?"

"No indeed," said Damaris, who had come into the stable. "I for one am not ready to risk another explosion."

Lord Cardell gave an agitated squawk and tossed the covers back over his machine. "What are you doing here?" he demanded combatively.

"Don't worry, I have not come to spy on you," Damaris retorted. "I have come to feed the horses."

Realizing that Damaris was in truth carrying two heavy-looking buckets, Sinclair took them from her. "Where is your groom?" he wondered.

"We have not got one."

His lordship looked astonished, and Damaris felt her cheeks go warm. Of course, Lord Sinclair would be used to having a dozen grooms and undergrooms running to meet his every need, and his Hampshire stables must be full of blood horses.

Damaris wished that his lordship had come to visit them in the days when the house had hummed with comfort and welcome, when Papa and Mama and Edward were alive and there was no need to pinch pennies or work like drudges or to lie in order to earn four hundred pounds.

There was a constriction in her throat as she said, "I warned you, sir, that you would not care for our way of life."

Lord Cardell growled something under his breath. He, too, had seen Lord Sinclair's expression and resented it. He hated the sight of Damaris having to work like the meanest of scullery maids. Worse than that he hated the distress he heard in her voice.

When he thought that Sinclair might be looking down his aristocratic nose at Damaris, Lord Cardell's hackles rose. " 'When Adam delved and Eve span,' " he quoted grumpily, " 'who was then the serving man?' Work does no harm to anyone."

Without a word Sinclair carried the buckets over to his grays and began to feed them. Damaris tried to intervene, but to no avail. "What are you doing?" she protested. "You are our guest, sir, and not a hired hand."

She broke off as the twins came bursting into the stables. "Dami, you're wanted back at the house right away," Lancelot shouted. "Grandmama's having spasms."

"She's been asking for you," added Fiona as her twin strove for breath. "She says she wants to be buried in her wedding dress."

Sinclair looked alarmed, but Lord Cardell merely shrugged. "Don't regard it, my boy. Just one of Lucinda's starts. 'Struth. Woman's been at death's door at least twenty times."

Damaris did not stay to hear more of this medical history but picked up her skirts and ran for the house. The twins followed her, relating other catastrophes. Bowens had sprained his back while digging up the potatoes. "And Peter tried to help him and wrenched his ankle," Fiona panted. "It must have hurt, Dami, for he used language that made Hepzibah turn quite green. It's a good thing Grandmama did not hear him, or she would have had more spasms."

Lady Cardell did not look at all well when Damaris tapped on her bedroom door. "This comes from being forced to stand in the rain," she wheezed in a die-away voice. "I have caught my death, Damaris. Pray listen to me; when the time comes, I wish a high church funeral service. High church, mark. The other is so vulgar."

It took a full ten minutes before Damaris could soothe the old lady, persuade her to lie down with her feet up, and sip the hot peppermint tisane that Harriet brought her. Another quarter of an hour passed before she allowed that *perhaps* she might try one piece of buttered toast.

"How is Peter?" Damaris asked Hetty as the two tiptoed out of the sickroom.

"His ankle has swollen up like a ball. I am persuaded that he must not walk on it for at least a day." Harriet made a wry face. "What a case of pickles this is, Dami. But don't disasters always come in threes?"

The third misfortune was soon to manifest itself. Hepzibah served breakfast looking so pale that Damaris was concerned. "It's naething at all," Hepzibah insisted, but when pressed, admitted lugubriously to a "small, wee, headache. It will go away if I lie doon," she added.

But it did not go away, and Damaris put her to bed with a cold compress.

Damaris was certain that Lord Sinclair would now take to his heels, but she had underestimated her man. His lordship not only stayed on but also made himself extremely useful.

Torn between her grandmother's tyrannies and the task of organizing and running the household, Damaris found Lord Sinclair's support was nothing short of a miracle. Who else but a worker of wonders, she asked Hetty later, could have organized the men of the household?

Lord Sinclair set the agitated old gardener to peeling potatoes, put Peter in charge of little Belle, galvanized the twins into dusting and sweeping. He had even—and this, Damaris considered incredible—got Lord Cardell to leave off working on his Wonder long enough to walk the horses while he, Sinclair, mucked out the stables.

Without his lordship, Damaris admitted, she could not have managed. She told him so later during a simple supper of shepherd's pie, and he smiled up at her. "No need to thank me. I'm enjoying being useful."

To his own considerable surprise, Sinclair meant what he said. After weeks of idleness at Pardom, he was finding it actually pleasant to work with his hands. The ennui that had shadowed his days disappeared under the unfamiliar physical labor, and there was a different ring to his voice, a new light in his eye. Peter, who made no bones of being thoroughly impressed by his lordship, said that he was like a general marshaling his troops.

"But that's natural," he added respectfully. "You were an officer in the war, weren't you, sir? And decorated at Waterloo. No wonder you've taken charge of us all."

Sinclair merely smiled, but Damaris noted the sudden shadows in his eyes and understood the cause. Before Peter could say more about Waterloo, she spoke in a matter-of-fact tone. "We must make a decision. Shall we have potatoes or turnips for tomorrow's dinner?"

As he listened to the Cardells discussing the merits of these vegetables, Sinclair watched Damaris. In the past days he had formed a new respect for her tact and good sense as well as for her ability to turn her hand to almost any task, and now his fine lips twisted dryly as he considered her brother. He could not see that gentleman bathing Lady Cardell's forehead in lavender water, mopping up the kitchen, cooking and carrying slops. Most of all he could not see Winter, with his fine-fitting clothes and easy charm, make light of hardship and the general work which, Sinclair feared, might prove too much for Damaris.

Fortunately, the Cardells were a tough lot. The dowager rallied on the third day, Hepzibah wheezed to her feet, and Peter's sprain mended. Even so, Lord Sinclair continued to work hard. Damaris, on her way to pick some more peppermint for Lady Cardell's tisane, found him digging up turnips under Bowens's direction and stopped to admire them.

"They're a good size," his lordship agreed. "Bigger than the ones I dug up at home when I was a boy." He smiled into her astonished face. "I've done this sort of thing before, Madam Mystery. My father believed that work was honorable, so my sisters and I each had our chores."

Damaris regarded his lordship with even more interest and respect. "Does he still require such heroics of you?"

"He's dead. Both he and my mother." Damaris noted that Lord Sinclair's eyes held a contemplative glow. "A pity, for you would have enjoyed knowing one other."

And Edward would have liked you. As the thought touched her mind, Lord Sinclair changed the subject. "What would you do if you could have anything you wanted?" he asked.

Damaris thought of wishing the past undone, of having Mama and Papa and Edward alive again, of having enough money to feed the household. But these were things that did not bear thinking of, let alone discussion with Lord Sinclair, so she made a light answer.

"I would like to go to the harvest fair." He looked interested, so she explained, "There is always a fair at this time of year, held on the town green. Merchants and musicians and sideshows come from all over to show strange sights and spread their wares. There are contest of skill and speed and—oh, so many things. I would like it above all things if I could take the children there."

"Well, why don't you?"

"It is not possible, really. The fair will be held tomorrow, and Hepzibah cannot take care of Lady Cardell by herself. And anyway, we have no—" Damaris checked herself. "We have no time."

She had meant to say that she had no money. Sinclair looked thoughtful, went away after luncheon, and was gone for some time. When he returned, he had with him two competent-looking middle-aged women and three strong young men.

"I have been to the village," he announced. "This is Mrs. Boom, who is reputed to be an excellent cook, and this is Margery, who will clean the house and see to the invalids. Tom and Perry here will assist Bowens, and Clancy will take care of the horses."

Damaris was astonished into blunt speech. "But we can't afford these people."

"They've already been paid for a day's work, so they should earn it. It is," Lord Sinclair stated, "the least I could do to express my gratitude for your hospitality."

"That is fudge, sir, and we both know it. What hospitality?"

"You've treated me as one of the family. I have enjoyed myself, and now I want to settle my debt."

Damaris began to protest, but he put his fingers lightly on her lips to silence her. The touch of his fingers on her mouth lasted only a fraction of a second, yet in that brief space of time, Damaris felt as though her ordered world had shifted. It was incredible that a brief, cool touch could cause such confusion.

"Listen," Lord Sinclair said.

The air was filled with excited shouts and laughter. Lancelot was telling Fiona about the two-headed sheep and the bearded woman and the strongest man in the world. Peter pretended that he was far too old for such diversions and then allowed that he should go along to protect his sisters. Belle clapped her hands and danced, singing that she was going, too. Even Hetty, always so quiet and sensible, came running out to throw her arms around Damaris and cry, "Dami, can we *really* afford to go to the fair?"

Hetty's face was flushed, her eyes bright with excitement. Damaris did not have the heart to tell her and her other siblings that they could not go. "You must let me pay you back," she sternly informed Lord Sinclair, "or else I will not agree to it."

The younger Cardells continued to talk about the fair all day, and at supper Mrs. Boom's stewed chicken with herbed dumplings and ginger fool made quite a sensation. Old Lord Cardell devoured three helpings of the pudding and professed himself indebted to Sinclair.

"Good idea, giving the children a treat," he enthused. "Used to enjoy the fair myself when I was a boy. Won first prize in a race, once, 'struth!"

"Why not come with us tomorrow, sir?" Sinclair asked.

Lord Cardell looked surprised, then pleased, and then thoughtful. "No," he said, "don't believe I will. Youth and crabbed age, you know. Have a better time without me, 'struth."

"And it is such a *rural* event," the dowager sniffed. She had risen from her sickbed as soon as she learned that Lord Sinclair had hired servants, and had hugely enjoyed finding fault with everything they did. "Believe me, Lord Sinclair, you will be wishing yourself home before you spend an hour in that place."

Lord Cardell said nothing, but Damaris noted that there was an odd gleam in his eye. "I am sure that Grandpapa wants to go to the fair," she told Harriet later. "He is too afraid of Grandmama's tongue to say so. It is too bad."

The twins did not get much sleep that night, for Lancelot had heard that it might rain, and Fiona and he were up every half hour to check the weather. Their fears notwithstanding, the day dawned fair and mild, and since the fair was to be held not more than a mile from Cardell House, it was decided that the party proceed on foot.

"We'll do this in style," Sinclair decreed. "First the twins, then Miss Harriet and Belle and Peter."

Harriet held her arms out for Belle, but Damaris shook her head. "I will carry her today."

Sinclair realized that she wanted Harriet and Peter to be free to enjoy themselves. "It will be a family outing," he agreed, "very proper."

Damaris was not so sure about propriety. There seemed something intimate about walking next to his lordship. Belle, who insisted on being carried by Lord Sinclair, looked so pretty that people stopped to smile at them. Damaris heard one lady say, "What a charming young couple. Can all those redheaded children be theirs?"

She glanced at Lord Sinclair and saw that he was grinning. He looked so young and carefree that Damaris's heart took wing. She felt as though the hard years had dropped away and that she was without a worry in the world. In fact, she was almost tempted to skip as the twins were doing.

As they approached the fairgrounds, excitement grew. "Oh, sir!" Lancelot breathed, his eyes bright and shining. "Can we see the living skeleton? And the two-headed sheep? And look, there is a man who can swallow fire. Can we see *him*, too?"

Their progress was joyful but slow. Belle snuggled trustingly in Sinclair's arms with a circle of barley-sugar he bought for her. Fiona, hand in hand with Damaris, looked about her with wide eyes while Lancelot, Harriet, and even Peter explored and stared and giggled like small children.

Lord Sinclair insisted on paying for everything and treating everyone. He then joined Damaris as she explored every sight, investigated every booth. "This reminds me," he said as they stopped at a ribbon seller's stall, "of a time when our head groom's son and I slipped out and went to the fair.

We had a few pence each to spend, and we got sick on pork pies. It was a wonderful day."

"It *is* a wonderful day," she amended softly. "I thank you for it."

"The pleasure is entirely mine, Madam Mystery."

She smiled at the foolish name. They were standing very close together; her lips were soft, and her eyes were sparkling. Sinclair found himself holding his breath and fighting a sudden, lunatic desire to lean forward and kiss Damaris Winter.

"Dami, Lord Sinclair!" Lancelot was racing toward them, his face as bright as his hair. "I've entered the race for eight-year-old boys. Come and see me win the piglet!"

Damaris was not sorry that her brother had come when he did. There had been something in Lord Sinclair's expression that made her feel lightheaded, and even now she felt a little unbalanced. She did not meet his lordship's eyes as they followed Lancelot to the site of the race, where a respectable crowd had gathered.

Peter, Harriet, and Fiona were waiting there. "Look at the piglet, Dami," Peter urged. "Won't it produce pork and bacon someday!"

The Cardells eyed the pig with hope and respect. Lancelot looked determined to do his best as he took his place at the starting line, but so did the other contestants. Damaris noted that one poorly dressed boy, taller and stronger-looking than the other runners, kept his eyes on the prize pig.

The race started and the Cardells jumped up and down as they cheered for Lancelot. Little Belle, standing beside Fiona, shouted the loudest. Sinclair found himself cheering, too, as the redhead took the lead.

Suddenly the big youth Damaris had seen earlier made a supreme effort. He sprinted forward and bumped Lancelot so hard that the smaller boy went head over heels.

"Foul!" Damaris cried, but her voice was drowned out by the noise everyone was making. A moment later, the big boy had won the race.

Sinclair strode over to Lancelot and helped him to his feet. "You should have won," he declared grimly. "I'm going to tell the judges to disqualify that cheat."

Damaris glared at the boy who had cheated, and he glared back over the pig he held. His eyes were fierce, but his hands looked chapped and sore, and as she saw those hands, Damaris's indignation ebbed. The boy was poor, and from the look of him, he had no one to care for him or even mend his clothes.

"Do you really want that to happen, Lancelot?" she asked, gently. "Do you want the boy disqualified?"

Lancelot followed Damaris's gaze, and his own indignation seemed to ebb. He turned to Lord Sinclair, saying, "Please, sir, don't do anything. He looks as if he needs the pig more than we do. We're all right, you know."

Sinclair watched the way the Cardells drew close to Damaris, who put her arms around as many of them as she could. He saw Fiona take her twin's hand while Harriet touched Lancelot's cheek and Peter put his hand on his brother's shoulder. In that moment the Cardells seemed very rich indeed.

Once again, Sinclair's instincts warred with the suspicions that had taken him to London. He *had* to be wrong about the Winters, he thought.

He spoke heartily to dispel this thought. "Well, Lancelot, you shall choose where we go next. Will we visit the fireproof man with his feet in boiling tar? Or would you like to go to that big tent and see the play *Death Comes for Ali Kafam*, or *The Turkish Horror*?"

Lancelot decided on the play, and by the time it was over, twilight had fallen and stars were glinting in the sky. As they stood at the entrance of the tent, they could hear the cheerful sound of fiddles playing. A large space had been ringed with lanterns, and within that ring men and women were hopping energetically in a country dance.

"What fun," Harriet exclaimed. "Peter, let's join them."

Peter turned brick red, jammed his hands in his pockets, and begged his sister to take a damper. Undaunted, Harriet caught Damaris's hands and pulled her into the ring.

Together the sisters hopped and skipped and sang along to the tune played by the fiddlers. But when she and Hetty swung away to find a new partner, Damaris found herself face-to-face with Lord Sinclair.

There was no time for surprise, for words, or even for thought before Damaris was being spun about in his lordship's arms. Then they hopped together, linked hands, and skipped around the torchlit ring.

When she moved, Sinclair thought, Damaris's flower fragrance danced along with her. And though it was time for them to separate and seek new partners, he could not make himself let go of the small, capable hands he held.

Instead, he pulled Damaris out of the ring of dancers. "It's getting too crowded in there," he said.

She did not protest but began to clap her hands to the music. From where they stood, they could see that the twins had joined the dance. Baby Belle, in Peter's arms, was watching and clapping, too.

"What a lovely night," Damaris murmured.

The happiness in her voice reached deep into Sinclair and reminded him of a time before the madness of war, a time when there had been pleasure in music and laughter, Sinclair tried to shake his head clear of mist and moonshine, but could not do so. Not when Damaris looked up at him with that expression in her eyes.

No woman, his lordship thought dazedly, had the right to have eyes as black as midnight and lips as soft as a pomegranate flower.

"Yes," he agreed. "Lovely."

His voice was husky, his face limned against the dark. In the shadows, his hard profile seemed softened, and the line of his mouth was tender. The expression in his eyes made Damaris catch her breath.

She knew that he was going to kiss her. She wanted him to. Damaris closed her eyes as his lordship lowered his lips to hers. Music and noise drifted away, smoke and the crackle of torches ebbed, and all she could hear was the beat of Lord Sinclair's heart. All she could feel was the firm, sweet pressure of his lips on hers.

Then into this magical world intruded a thundering, explosive noise. It was as though all the thunderbolts in the sky had let loose at once, and sparks of flame and billows of steam tormented the torchlit darkness. There were shrieks and howls of "It's them anarchists!" and "Murder!" and one man insisted that Napoleon had come back to invade England.

Damaris pulled free of Lord Sinclair's arms. "Belle! Fiona!" she screamed. "Where are you?"

As if in answer, a monster shape materialized out of the darkness. It lumbered forward, groaned, and seemed to hesitate.

"Oh, confound it." Lord Cardell's anguished voice wafted through the sudden silence. "Oh, go *on*, you useless heap of nuts and bolts."

Sinclair and Damaris stared with the rest as Lord

Cardell's Wonder creaked into the torchlight, wheezed, and died.

"Scragged," shouted his lordship. "Done for. Bloody well dished up by a damned nincompoop of a machine!"

Chapter Seven

It took a hired cart and four nervous horses an hour to haul Lord Cardell's Wonder back to the house. The task was made more onerous by the owner of the cart, who demanded an exorbitant fee for dragging around a contraption that, as he put it, could explode at any moment. He grumbled until Lord Sinclair appeased him by offering to lead the horses.

Sinclair could not help grinning whenever he thought of the Wonder's untimely appearance, but the Cardell family obviously considered the machine's debut a tragedy. A dismal Peter took charge of his equally glum brothers and sisters, whilst Damaris walked beside her grandfather and attempted to console him.

Lord Cardell was mired fast in gloom. "Been planning this for months," he groaned. "Spent a lot of blunt on new pipes and such. Thought if people saw what the Wonder could do, an investor would get word of it and our fortune would have been made."

He glared at his invention. "It was the valve again—damn thing got stuck and pressure built up. Oh, Lucinda's going to rake me over the coals!"

He was a true prophet. No sooner had they returned to Cardell House but the dowager advanced upon them and called on God and man to witness how she had been victimized for years by an Unfeeling Man who endangered and beggared himself and his family. She carried on until Lord Cardell flew into a passion, shouted that she was a foolish bag of moonshine, then retreated into the stables, banged the doors shut, and locked himself in.

"No, I won't come out," he yelled out of the keyhole at Damaris, who was attempting to reason with him. "Only place a man can get any peace. Go away and let me alone."

Sinclair, who was torn between mirth and a real sympathy for the old fellow's woes, told Damaris not to worry. "He needs time to lick his wounds," he said. "After a while he'll cheer up and remind himself that scientific progress has its ups and downs. There's no need to be so anxious."

There was a caring, almost caressing note in his deep voice that confused Damaris. Until now she had been too busy to remember what Lord Cardell's appearance had interrupted.

"I must go back to the others," she said.

But she did not want to go back to the house. What Damaris wanted more than anything else was to walk into Lord Sinclair's arms. She wanted to rest her cheek against his broad shoulder and be held as tightly as she had been held earlier tonight. She wanted to lift her lips for his kiss—

"Don't go," Lord Sinclair said.

Moon-madness rushed back into Damaris's veins. Her knees felt weak as though her bones were beginning to turn soft. "No one needs you at the moment," Sinclair continued. "Lady Cardell is brooding in the morning room. The children and Miss Harriet are having bread and milk and telling Hepzibah about their day."

As he spoke, he took Damaris's hands in his. They seemed to tremble in his clasp, and her sudden vulnerability filled him with inexplicable emotions. He wanted to put his arms around her and protect her. He wanted to sweep her into his arms and kiss her breathless.

With the magic of remembered lamplight and music swirling in his brain, Sinclair spoke softly. "You worry too much about other people. For once think of yourself, Damaris Winter."

Damaris *Winter*.

Damaris felt as though she had been slapped. The warm note in Lord Sinclair's voice was not for her—it was for the fictional Miss Winter. If he realized what lies she had been living, he would certainly not continue to smile at her in that way.

It was useless now to bring up the shopworn arguments that she needed to feed her family. Damaris felt wretched and wicked.

Pulling her hands away from his lordship's clasp, she said, "I *must* go back to the house."

In an effort to douse the hen-hearted quiver in her voice, she spoke quite sternly, and her repressive tones recalled Sinclair suddenly and rudely to reality. All at once he remembered why he had gone to London and what he was doing in Kent.

Was he mad, Sinclair wondered, or merely moonstruck? It was the only explanation for his extraordinary behavior. That, and the fact that Damaris Winter had nestled into his arms as though she had been made for that purpose. Even now, with his sanity rapidly reasserting itself, he wanted nothing more than to hold her close to him.

Lord Sinclair locked his hands firmly behind his back and forced himself to speak in a brisk tone.

"Perhaps you are right. I've also been thinking," he added after a moment, "that it's time I returned to Pardom. The emergency seems to be over at Cardell House, so perhaps you wish to drive back with me tomorrow?"

Even as Damaris's heart sank, she recognized the sense of what his lordship was saying. She knew that she could no longer put off her departure now that the family needed money more than ever.

Accordingly, she and Lord Sinclair journeyed back to Sussex next day. Neither of them were inclined to make small conversation, and their journey was largely a silent one. But as his lordship's curricle drove up to the door, a sharp crack sounded from the garden.

"Heavens," Damaris exclaimed, "what was that?"

"Pistol shot," Sinclair replied curtly. He dismounted, tossed the reins to a groom, and snapped, "Stay here."

Ignoring him, Damaris jumped to the ground and hastily followed Lord Sinclair into the gardens. "Oh, heavens!" she exclaimed.

A body was lying on the ground. Half of it was concealed by the branches of a low-growing shrub, but the lower torso, with its stout legs, bottle green corduroy pantaloons, and silver-buckled shoes, was unmistakable.

"Uncle Molyneux, is that you?" Sinclair demanded sternly.

The "body" twitched, then heaved itself to a sitting position. "Curse it, Nicholas," the earl complained, "this is the second time you've spoiled things."

Damaris stared wide-eyed as Ambrose Garland came strolling around the topiary hedge. He had a smoking pistol in his hand. "Welcome back, Damaris," he said. "And you, too, Lord Sinclair."

"Where did you get that pistol?" Sinclair demanded.

Garland gave the weapon a spin. "The earl lent it to me so that we could work out a scene from the book."

"Surely you don't intend to act out every chapter," Sinclair exclaimed irritably. "How close is the confounded thing to being finished?"

"It won't be long now that I have my assistant back," Garland replied.

Damaris wanted to scream. She had hated the deceptions and the lies from the beginning, and the events of the past few days had made her hate them even more. She wished that she could unburden herself here and now and confess the truth.

As if he had read her thoughts, Garland went on, "I hope that your going to Cardell House averted a crisis, Damaris. The family depends upon you *so* much."

He took her arm and began to walk with her toward the house. "I'm truly glad you're back," he added in a low voice. "That man's got mice in his cockloft. I was idiot enough to tell him part of the plot—that Sir Cuthbert tries to kill Lord Tedell—and Pardom thinks he should be shot in the garden. He insists that Tedell be left bleeding under the chestnut tree."

"That has been done before," she replied mechanically. "I had Lord Tedell shot in *The Duke's Portrait.*"

"What will it be, then? A knife in the dark, a fall, a twist of the garrote?"

Damaris clenched her hands. "I wish," she cried, "that I had never heard of Lord Tedell."

Garland made soothing noises. "Tell me about your visit home," he said. "How are the children? Is Lord Cardell any closer to selling one of his inventions?"

Damaris told him about the debut of Lord Cardell's Wonder machine, and Garland laughed heartily. "You have had an exciting time!" he exclaimed. "I'm surprised that Sinclair made himself so agreeable, though. He certainly was in a black mood when he rode off to Kent. Your family must have charmed him into good humor."

Damaris did not want to discuss his lordship. "Has Liza returned from her visit to Miss Neece?" she asked.

"She came back today." Garland made a wry face. "I don't think there's any cause to worry, by the way. That young lady hasn't even looked at me since you left for Kent."

Damaris went back to work as soon as she had unpacked. She worked through the afternoon and was still writing when Nancy came to help her dress for dinner.

The abigail was full of gossip. The house had been quiet with Lady Liza gone to Neece Place, but no one had missed the accompanying Miss Fuffletter. "Eh, but she gives me the shivers, ma'am, wi' her whinings and sneakings, and her airs about her wonderful cousin Lady Armstrother. Why doesn't she go live with my lady if she likes her so much?" Nancy paused. "And that Lady Freemont were here again. She's interested in Mr. Winter."

Damaris, who had been listening with half an ear, looked up at this. "What did you say, Nancy?"

"Nay, it's as plain as the nose on my face, ma'am. Lady Freemont's been neighbor to the master for twenty year, but only now does she come visiting." Nancy nodded wisely. "Happen she thinks that a literary gentleman'd raise her standing in the eyes of them Sussex Muses she belongs to. She wants Mr. Winter to be her pro-tay-jay as the Frenchies say."

The proof of this awaited Damaris downstairs.

When she came into the drawing room, where they usually gathered to await a summons for dinner, she found the earl glowering at a card in his hand.

"Curst bore," he was growling. "Been living near the Freemonts for years. Never bothered me before this."

Damaris sent an inquiring look at Garland, who explained, "Lady Freemont has graciously invited us to an assembly at her home."

"Nothing gracious about it," retorted his patron. "Curst boring affair, with boring people and boring conversation. Your fault, Winter. Lady F. wants to show you off to her curst poets. Still, they're neighbors, so I suppose we can't cry off."

Liza tossed her head. "Well, *I* am not going. I don't like the Freemonts."

"You'll do as you're told," the earl snapped, and when Liza protested, lost his temper and bade her keep a civil tongue in her head. "You've been a plague and a disappointment to me all m'life," he shouted at her.

Liza burst into tears and ran out of the room. "What's the matter with the chit?" the earl demanded. "You," he added to Miss Fuffletter, "go after her and see what ails her. Why did I ever have a daughter? She's more curst trouble than she's worth."

Lord Sinclair looked up sharply, but before he could speak, Damaris cried, "How can you say such a thing? She is only growing up."

The earl scowled at her. "Hey?" he growled. "What slum are you spouting?"

Holding her temper, Damaris said evenly, "Liza is a young woman, sir. She is almost seventeen."

"Tchah," snapped the earl. "Who asked for *your* opinion?"

"It is easy to say 'tchah,' " Damaris retorted with energy, "but the problem will not go away. Liza has played the part of a hoyden because she knows you wanted a son, and it amused you to see her climb trees and hear her talk cant. But now she has outgrown these things. She cannot climb trees and act like a hey-go-mad lad forever."

The earl stared at her openmouthed. No one save Arabella Neece, who had known him since they were in leading strings and had always been uncomfortably outspoken, had ever addressed him in such a tone.

Damaris disregarded the empurpling of the earl's cheeks. "It is perhaps time, my lord," she said sternly, "that you started to think more about your daughter and less of yourself. To tell her that she is a disappointment to you is not only untrue but cruel."

Miss Fufletter, who had been walking toward the door, turned her head and stared. Sinclair looked thoughtful. Garland, who had been listening in mounting horror as Damaris spoke, suggested that his sister was not herself. "The long journey from Kent must have brought on a fever," he said.

Damaris began to reply that she felt exceedingly well but then realized that her stomach was churning. With as much dignity as she could muster, she excused herself and left the room. Miss Fufletter scurried after her.

"Oh, my *dear* Miss Winter, how unfortunate," she twittered. "That you should *dare* to anger the earl. But you are far braver than I am. You are not afraid of anything, are you? You are what my cousin Lady Amstrother would call a nonpareil!"

She swayed back and forth, and her pale eyes flickered with malice. She made no bones of the fact that she was glad that Damaris was in trouble and would surely be dismissed by the earl.

And without her, Mr Garland could not write the book—but there was no use crying over spilled milk.

Damaris squared her shoulders and, walking briskly up the stairs, tapped on Liza's door.

Liza was standing by the open window looking out and did not even look around when Damaris came in. "I suppose you are going to tell me I must go to the Freemont woman's party," she charged. "Well, I won't."

"Suit yourself," Damaris replied. She went to Liza's wardrobe and flung it open.

Liza whipped about to exclaim, "What are you doing?"

"I am looking at your dresses," Damaris replied. "It is a good thing that you have made up your mind not to go to that party, Liza, for you have nothing suitable to wear."

"Lady Lizabeth need not go to that woman's house," snuffled Miss Fuffletter, who had followed Damaris into Liza's room. "She need not suffer humiliation and grief."

"If she is dressed in these odious clothes, she deserves to suffer." Damaris lifted out an ugly round-dress with grass stains on the hem. "Liza, you are every bit as pretty as Miss Freemont. What a pity you do not have the courage to put her to the blush."

Liza scowled. "You mean that I'm fighting shy?"

Damaris met the indignant, red-rimmed eyes. "Aren't you?" she asked.

"How dare you?" Liza shouted. "I have never ratted in my life. Devil fly off, Damaris, I am not sheep-hearted."

Damaris simply shrugged.

"I'll show you!" Liza swung around from the window. "I will have a new dress made and go to that damned party."

"Lady *Lizabeth*," gasped her governess. "Your *language*." She turned to Damaris. "It is your fault, Miss Winter. You encourage her."

She tottered from the room, and Liza turned to Damaris. A small, hopeful smile curved her lips. "Am I really as pretty as Miss Freemont?" she whispered.

Damaris hugged her, hard. "Prettier," she replied. "Much, *much* prettier. You will see, Liza. You will be a diamond of the first water, and the Freemonts will expire from envy."

It was a sop to Damaris's conscience that she could at least help Liza emerge from her chrysalis before she was dismissed from Pardom. But though she expected the order of her expulsion momentarily, it did not come. Next morning at breakfast the earl seemed subdued and only grunted noncommittally when his daughter announced her intention to go to the Freemont party after all.

But when breakfast was over, he paused at Damaris's side to growl, "Your doing, hey? You've got spirit—got to give you that."

He took himself off, and Damaris, staring after the earl's hastily retreating back, did not observe the look Miss Fuffletter turned on her or the quick clawing movement of the governess's hands.

Aloud she simpered, "*Dear* Miss Winter, you are so clever. Have you decided what Lady Lizabeth is to wear?"

Damaris thought she understood the whine in the governess's voice. The lank, unlovely Miss Fuffletter was worried about her position. Her pretensions to being a well-connected lady's cousin were merely her way of disguising her deep insecurity.

With this in mind, Damaris did her best to defer to the governess's judgment, but unfortunately, the woman had horrible taste. She suggested a pink tarlatan evening dress strewn with silk roses, which was completely unsuitable, and jewels that would have made Liza look too old. As diplomatically as possible, Damaris offered alternatives, and fortunately, Liza listened.

Damaris herself had not planned to go to the Freemonts'. She had hoped that with everyone out of the house, she could work in peace. But Liza threatened that she would not set foot on Freemont property without Damaris's support, and Garland seconded this.

"How would it look," he pointed out, "if I accepted the invitation and left you home? Pardom insists on my attending the Freemonts' assembly, so I'm afraid you have to go, too."

He paused and sent her a wry smile. "Living at Pardom has its difficult moments. I hope that the book will be finished soon."

"I am trying," Damaris replied, meekly. "It is just this problem of that attempt on Lord Tedell's life. I wish I could fix on some method that is out of the ordinary. Something that will catch my imagination."

On the night of the Freemonts' party, Damaris put on her one passable dress, a deep bronze tarlatan. It suited her well enough, and she tried to pretend that the fashionable Freemonts would not recognize its age. Fortunately, Damaris had no time to dwell on the matter, for Liza's debut was all-important. She and Nancy, with Miss Fuffletter hovering about like a dissatisfied moth, joined forces to bring out the young girl's piquant beauty.

They spent hours on the effort, but it was worth it to see the earl's face when his daughter came hesitantly down the circular stairs.

Liza had been transformed. Her fair hair was carefully combed and brushed back into a fall of curls. Her dress was simple, as suited a maiden who had not yet had her come-out, but the rosy crepe flattered Liza's skin and her slender curves. A necklace of small but perfectly matched pearls gave her neck delicacy.

The earl was speechless. For a moment he stared at his daughter, then turned hastily away. Sinclair, who had been standing behind his uncle, saw to his astonishment that there were tears in Pardom's eyes.

"Looks like her mother," the earl grated. Then, recovering, he coughed loudly and wondered why it took curst females so long to deck themselves out.

"Well done, Liza," Sinclair murmured as his uncle walked unsteadily apart and pretended to examine an ugly portrait on the wall.

Then he saw Damaris. With inborn tact, she had stayed back and let Liza descend by herself. Sinclair noted that Damaris wore her magnificent hair in a simple knot at the back of her head and that he had seen her bronze dress at least once before. But her smile was radiant, full of happiness at the effect Liza was having.

Standing on a table in the hall was a bowlful of late roses. Sinclair selected two—a creamy rosebud and a tea rose. He carried the flowers to the stairs and bowed.

"My lady," he said, presenting the white rosebud to Liza.

Damaris felt a lump in her throat as Liza blushed prettily and said, "Thank you, Cousin Nicholas," in a young, soft voice.

"I think thanks are due somewhere else." Sinclair turned to Damaris with a smile and gave her an even deeper bow. "Ma'am, my homage."

As she took the rose he offered her, her fingers brushed his. That shadow-touch caused Damaris's heart to beat faster. There was no reason for it—none at all—except that Lord Sinclair was looking down at her with such pleasure that she felt her heart grow light.

"Are we going to stand around sniffing curst flowers all night?" demanded the earl irascibly. He was wishing that he had presented Liza with the rose himself, and that made him more irritable than usual. "Ah, there you are, Winter. About time you got here."

Sinclair saw that, in contrast to his sister's modest and obviously well-worn gown, Desmond Winter was dressed in the kick of fashion. His long-tailed coat of blue superfine, his well-fitting fawn breeches, and his handsome waistcoat embroidered with silver flowers would have done justice to any dandy. Beside him, Damaris Winter looked like a poor relation.

How could siblings be so different? Sinclair wondered as the earl's party took their places in the carriage. He himself shared many character traits with his sisters, and while they did not precisely look like one another, there was a definite family resemblance. But Winter and his sister not only did not look anything like each other, they were poles apart in everything they did.

Even now, as the earl's carriage rattled through a stone gate flanked by lions, Winter was sitting up and looking about him with interest and appreciation, while his sister seemed sunk in a brown study. What was she thinking? Sinclair wondered, then saw her touch the rose he had given her.

Damaris was wondering what was causing her to act in such a caper-witted way. She had not wanted to come to the Freemonts', and yet when Lord Sinclair handed her that rose and looked at her in *that* way, her heart had seemed to shiver into excitement and anticipation.

Anticipation about what? Damaris asked herself as the carriage stopped before an imposing house built in the last century. Here the marble steps had been carpeted in crimson, and footmen in liveries as crimson as the carpet ran about, letting down the steps of carriages, barouches, and phaetons. There was a great deal of affected laughter and greetings bandied back and forth as the Quality girded its loins to endure another of the Freemonts' country parties.

Liza looked about her with round eyes. "Devil fly off, Damaris, this is a ball, not an assembly. I'm not suitably dressed."

"You look beautiful, Liza," Damaris encouraged. "Everyone will think so."

"Not Caroline Freemont," replied Liza. "That cat will be dressed to the nines and make me look like a homely Joan."

The Freemonts were on the spacious first-floor landing receiving their guests, and as Liza had predicted, both Lady Freemont and her daughter were gowned in the height of fashion. Lady Freemont wore a jade crepe ball dress embellished with velvet ribbons, and her daughter a silver gauze overdress atop a cream-colored slip of India silk. Jewels flashed in their hair, in their décolletage, and on their fingers. Damaris saw Ambrose Garland's eyes gleam with admiration as he kissed Miss Freemont's hand.

"Oh, Lady Lizabeth, how charming you look," Lady Freemont murmured in her languid way. Then she turned to more interesting game. "I *hope*, Mr. Winter, that you will not look down your nose at us provincial poets."

"Madam," the supposed writer said gallantly, "if I was such a churl, I would deserve to be horsewhipped."

Damaris watched a shadow of distaste cross Sinclair's face, but she had no time to refine on it, for Lady Freemont had turned to her. "Miss Winter, how good of you to come. What a charming dress, to be sure. It reminds me of one I had made in London some seasons ago."

Damaris was human enough to feel hurt by the unfeeling words. She had just been reminded that she was a hireling, here on sufferance because her brother was Pardom's protégé. The feeling of excitement withered within her, and she felt dreary and out of place.

Silently she followed the others in her party into the Freemonts' imposing drawing room, where the guests were gathered. Here Damaris's senses were assaulted by an excess of color, light, and perfume, for the walls were covered with mirrors that reflected the light of innumerable candelabras, and wreaths of flowers hung everywhere. Their cloying scent was oppressive.

Perhaps this heavy atmosphere explained the fact that no one was talking very much. In the group nearest to them, several exquisitely dressed ladies were conversing boredly with equally well-dressed but disinterested-looking gentlemen. As Damaris watched, a middle-aged lady in a white satin slip dress suddenly raised a hand to her flower-crowned brow, let the other hand rest lightly on her hip, tilted her head dramatically, and closed her eyes.

"What is the matter with her?" Liza wondered. "Is she going to faint?"

"No, no," Lady Freemont drawled. "Miss Jarris is merely striking an attitude. Those ladies and gentlemen are among the Sussex Muses, the group of poets of whom I am—shall I admit it?—secretary." She gave an affected laugh and tapped her fan on Garland's arm. "Mr. Winter, pray let me introduce you to the Muses."

As she led the supposed writer away, Lord Freemont, a dyspeptic, nervous-looking individual, appeared and engaged the earl and Lord Sinclair in conversation. This left Damaris and Liza to look blankly at each other.

"I feel," Liza whispered, "like a frog out of water. These ladies must spend all their time trying to decide what to wear. Is that what being a lady means?"

"I wish I knew." But Damaris was interrupted by a clear voice calling her name. "There is Miss Neece," she exclaimed gratefully.

Miss Neece, looking like a no-nonsense thistle in a purple gown and turban of the same color, was seated with a select group by the fire. She greeted Damaris kindly, complimented Liza on her appearance, then turned the talk to horses and hunts until Liza was at her ease and chatting happily with the others.

"And how is Lord Tedell?" Miss Neece then asked Damaris.

"In a quandary," Damaris admitted.

"How so?" Miss Neece patted a chair beside her. "Sit down and tell me all. What? Did the silly fool get himself into some fix from which your brother can't extricate him?"

Responding to the genuine interest in Miss Neece's eyes, Damaris confessed, "We need to make an attempt on his life but have not decided what sort of an attempt."

Surprisingly, Miss Neece looked somber. "Fiction is much easier than life. You can order people around and kill 'em or reform 'em to suit the plot. What? Ain't like that in real life, Damaris. Take Siddons, for instance."

According to Miss Neece, Siddons had finally been forced to close his establishment. "Not because of anythin' I did—a tragedy occurred. One young fellow who frequented the gamin' hall and was at point-non-plus shot himself. Name of Widdersby."

Damaris recalled the fair young man with the desperate eyes. "Did he . . . die?" she faltered.

"No, but he is grievously wounded." Miss Neece looked even more grave. "Pardom thinks me an interferin' old trout for ruinin' his fun, but I've seen what cards and dice can do. Young fellow I fancied in m'salad days gamed his inheritance away. Wasn't as lucky as Widdersby, unfortunately. Blew his brains out."

Damaris did not know what to say. Her heart was heavy for the young man and for Miss Neece, and also for her own father, who had been driven to take his life. "What a terrible world it is," she murmured.

Miss Neece put a hand on Damaris's shoulder for a moment. Then she said, "Mind you, all that happened a long time ago. What? Ain't been wearin' the willow all these years. In fact, could've marched into parson's mousetrap half a dozen times."

"But you did not."

"No need. I was always plump in the pockets and didn't want a husband. What? No desire to hand over my fortune to a man I didn't care for."

Damaris noted that Miss Neece was looking at Pardom. The earl was pointedly ignoring her.

"Then there was no one?" she could not help asking.

It was an impertinence, but Miss Neece did not seem to mind. She shook her head, and her intelligent eyes became shadowed with regret.

"Couldn't have the one I wanted," she said frankly. "Didn't want the ones I could have. No use chasin' rainbows, Damaris. And men can be baconbrained to a fault. What? They strut around and puff out their chests, but give them an emergency and they're all abroad. Take m'butler, Davidson. Man melted like butter when my maid got mushroom poisonin'. If I hadn't been there, the girl would be cockin' up her toes by now."

"Mushrooms," Damaris repeated softly. "Of course—mushrooms!"

Why had she not thought of it before? Lord Tedell was going to eat poisoned mushrooms. He was going to almost, but not *quite*, die from them.

"Can you tell me what kind of mushrooms your maid ate?" she asked hopefully.

Miss Neece frowned. "Well, that's hard to say. There's a lot of mushrooms about the countryside, what? Some of 'em are deucedly nasty customers."

Damaris listened, fascinated, as her companion explained that edible mushrooms like *Agaricus campestris* grew wild in pastures and meadows. "Wherever there's rich soil and manure. What? Good stuff, manure. Dependable. But then there's poisonous kinds which ain't so agreeable. Man sits down to his dish of mushrooms—say his silly ass of a cook's got hold of some of the deadly *Amanita* variety by mistake—and half an hour to two hours later, he's dizzy, can't see straight, and his bowels have turned to water."

It was on the tip of Damaris's tongue to ask what the *Amanita* mushrooms looked like when the musicians who had been playing outside on the landing entered the drawing room and arranged themselves in a corner. The floor was cleared, and Lady Freemont besought her guests to form sets for a cotillion.

There was a great deal of giggling as gentlemen sought out partners. A serious-looking young man—one of the Sussex Muses, Damaris noted—appeared and begged Liza for the honor of standing up with her, and a dowager in puce pulled up a chair close to Miss Neece and announced that she had been dying for a quiet cose with dear Arabella. Miss

Neece rolled her eyes and looked resigned, and Damaris silently slipped away.

She needed to go somewhere quiet and private so that she could write down the information Miss Neece had given her. She needed pen and paper. *"Amanita,"* Damaris whispered. *"Agaricus campestris."*

Muttering to herself, she stepped out of the drawing room and emerged on the wide and gleaming landing. Here she paused. She could hardly forage through every room in the house looking for pen and paper.

Damaris beckoned to an under-footman and desired that he bring her pen and paper and a room where she would not be disturbed. The footman was young enough to look astonished but sufficiently well trained to immediately do as she asked. A few minutes later, Damaris found herself in a small room off the drawing room. It was elegantly furnished with delicate white and gold furniture, works of art, and orchids blooming in jardinieres. Tall French windows had been opened to the evening, and the air was cool and fresh.

Damaris pulled a chair up to a gilt-edged desk, dipped her pen in ink, and began to write busily. Her mind flew before her fingers, and she began to murmur aloud to herself.

"The mushrooms will be in the stuffed grouse, I think. That would disguise the taste. The Earl of Brandon will have shot the grouse the day before, and Sir Cuthbert will have inserted the poisonous mushrooms when he—" Damaris stopped writing and exclaimed, "I *do* wish I knew how poison tastes."

"What's this about poison?"

She had been so engrossed in what she was writing that Damaris had not heard Lord Sinclair approach. Seeing him looking over her shoulder, she almost knocked over the ink bottle.

He rescued the ink bottle and nodded to the paper in front of her. "More research?" She nodded. "Don't you ever let it alone?"

Through the open door behind him were wafting sounds of music and dancing. "I am at Pardom to work," she reminded him. "The book must be finished if I am to go home again."

"You mean to Cardell House." She nodded. "Have you and your brother lived there all your lives?"

Damaris did not want to keep lying to him, and yet she was not sure how to extricate herself from a coil of falsehoods and half-truths. "We are very close," she hedged. "Since my oldest—*cousin*, Edward, was killed at Waterloo, things have been difficult for the Cardells."

"And so you have lived together since your cousin's death?"

Damaris felt as if she were becoming more and more mired in untruths. As she tried to think of something to say that would not incriminate her further, the orchestra struck up a spirited waltz.

"Do you waltz, Lord Sinclair?" she asked.

She had hoped to sidetrack him, but he only nodded absently, and she knew that he was about to ask her another unwanted question about the Cardells. Anxious to avoid that question, Damaris blurted, "Will you show me how it is done? It—it is research for the book. Cedric dances the waltz with Lady Hortensia, you see."

She looked so serious, and there was that familiar smudge of ink on her forefinger. She was irresistible. Feeling suddenly quite young and carefree and full of mischief, Sinclair slid an arm around Damaris's waist and began to waltz her about the room.

She had not forgotten how it had felt to be in his arms, but the memory had dimmed with time. Now, suddenly, Damaris's mind was tumbled back to that mad night. She found that she could hardly catch her breath—but perhaps that was because Lord Sinclair was holding her so tightly.

"My lord," she implored, "that is quite enough. I understand the principle of the waltz and I thank you, but . . . please stop," she begged as the skirt of her dress caught and toppled one of the fragile jardinieres. "This room is much too small to dance in, and we will smash all the flowers."

"You're quite right, we must think of the flowers," Sinclair replied, and promptly danced her out the French doors and into the garden beyond.

It was cool in the garden, and crickets were chirping forecasts of the winter to come. Trees swept velvet shadows across Damaris's cheeks and touched the corners of her mouth. The many candles that blazed from the house conspired to dazzle like reflected starlight in the depths of her eyes. It was, Sinclair thought, a little like looking into dark pools of water. A man could easily drown in such eyes.

"Are—are you foxed, my lord?" Damaris was asking. She sounded quite out of breath, and there was a faint quaver in her voice. "Are you feeling well?"

He had not touched a drop of spirits, and yet Sinclair felt almost giddy. He had no idea what madness had made him seize hold of Damaris and dance her outside like this, but he did not want to let her go.

Sinclair hardly realized that the moon was full and silver, or that a nightingale had begun to sing tenderly from a nearby bush. All that he knew was that he wanted—needed—to kiss the woman in his arms.

Damaris knew that Lord Sinclair meant to kiss her. Perhaps all this time she had been waiting for his kiss. And at the touch of his lips—sure and warm and sweet—the ground seemed to disappear under her feet and the firmament seemed to have gone mad around them both. Comets and shooting stars and galaxies of light blazed about her. And then she forgot everything but the reality of the strong arms that held her so close.

"Damaris," she heard him murmur against her mouth. "Damaris, my dear—"

"Really, Desmond? You think I'm prettier than Miss Freemont?"

The eager young voice came from the room from which they had just exited. Sinclair and Damaris sprang apart as Garland's voice wafted through the darkness toward them.

"What is Miss Freemont beside you? You are as lovely as the rose in your hair. When I saw you for the first time tonight, I thought you were a princess out of a fairy tale."

The darkness seemed to expand, to quiver with Liza's delighted sigh. "Oh, Desmond," she exclaimed, "*do* stop wasting time and kiss me!"

Chapter Eight

"Damnation!" Lord Sinclair roared. "Let go of my cousin before I break every bone in your body."

Liza gave a faint shriek. Garland whirled about, saw Sinclair come striding through the French doors toward him, and promptly dropped his arms from about Liza.

"This is not what it might seem. I assure you I have nothing but esteem for Liza—"

The rest of Garland's words were choked down his throat as his lordship seized him by his cravat. He made strangling noises, and Liza ran forward and pounded her fists on her cousin's broad back.

"You brute, Nicholas, let go of him! Damaris, make him let Desmond go."

Damaris's brain had seemed to go quite numb. She could only stammer, "Please do not do this. Think! You cannot want a scandal."

In the silence that followed her words, the sound of dancing and laughter seemed loud and very near. If he strangled Winter now, Sinclair realized, gossips would ruin Liza.

With an exclamation of disgust, he let his captive go. "I want you gone from Pardom tonight," he ordered.

"I'm your uncle's guest, not yours," Garland shot back. "If it's satisfaction you want—"

"I don't duel with your kind." Sinclair's voice stung like a whip. "You've abused my uncle's trust and attempted to seduce a girl not yet out of the schoolroom. You're below contempt."

"I beg you will stop this madness," Damaris pleaded. "Desmond, does—does this outrageous scene have something to do with your book?"

Both Liza and Garland seized on this excuse. "Oh, yes, that was it," Liza cried, and Garland said, "I was telling Lady Lizabeth about the young countess for whom Lord Tedell forms a tendre in the sixth chapter."

There was no such countess. Damaris felt miserable. "You were very wrong," she said. "Very wrong."

The unhappiness in her voice pierced Sinclair's fury. Though he still wanted to throttle Desmond Winter or at least expose him for the cad he was, he realized what would happen to Damaris if her precious brother were sent packing.

The supposed Winter was continuing smoothly, "If you had allowed me to explain, Lord Sinclair, I would have told you that Lady Lizabeth and I had been discussing *The Heir of Brandon Manor.* We could hardly hear ourselves think in the drawing room, so we came in here."

Distressed, Damaris exclaimed, "How could you be so indiscreet?"

"As indiscreet as your being outside with Sinclair, sister?"

The insolent cur—Sinclair's hands tightened into fists, but before he could act, there was the sound of footsteps outside and Pardom loomed in the doorway. "So there you are, Winter," he huffed.

Oblivious to the scene he had interrupted, the earl stumped into the room. "Lady Freemont sent me out to track you down. Wants to make you known to the Marchioness of Burforth. Got to warn you, boy, curst female's got some sonnets she wants to show you." He paused. "What, you here, too, Nicholas?"

Sinclair nodded wordlessly.

The earl surveyed the occupants of the room. "Just goes to show, don't it? Give a curst flat party and your guests do a bunk." He added regretfully, "Tempting to hide in here, but we'd better go back to the others. Freemont's going to announce dinner."

Damaris held her breath as she watched Lord Sinclair eye Garland. She half expected him to tell his uncle what had happened. Instead, he spoke quietly. "If you'll escort the ladies into the drawing room, sir, Winter and I will join you in a moment."

Liza sent her cousin a rebellious look but did not dare protest. As she and Damaris followed the earl into the drawing room, Sinclair turned to the man beside him.

No sane man could ignore the menace in that silent, gray gaze, and it was with an effort that Garland kept his voice steady. "What is it you want to say to me?"

"If I were to horsewhip you as you deserve," said Sinclair in a voice that matched his eyes, "Liza's name would be dragged through the mud. I'll say and do nothing for her sake. But from now on, every moment you spend at Pardom had better be used for writing."

Garland's handsome mouth was almost ugly with a sneer. "Anything else?"

"I give you," Sinclair continued icily, "one week

to finish that book. If during that time you so much as look at my cousin, I will thrash you like the cur you are."

He strode out of the room, overtaking Liza and Damaris just inside the drawing room. Liza glared at her tall cousin, but he only said, "I'll not have you act like a hoyden in public. Go sit down beside Miss Neece and try to act like a lady."

He walked away to join Pardom, and Liza clenched her small hands. "How *dare* he," she seethed. "Devil fly off, he is not my guardian."

No, Damaris thought, but Sinclair was a man of the world. He knew that people talked and that once a lady lost her reputation, it could be damaged forever. If one of the sharp-eyed, keen-nosed matrons in the drawing room had discovered what Lady Lizabeth was up to, it would soon be noised around town that Pardom's daughter was so hot at hand that she was like to tie her garter in public. And as for herself—

"It was not wise to be alone with him," Damaris muttered. "It was madness to go into his arms."

Liza misunderstood. "Damaris, it really did *begin* by being about the book. Des— Mr. Winter was explaining about how the Countess of Buckmanspire faints in Lord Tedell's arms. And then—"

She broke off, looking very young and a little frightened. "I really don't know what happened," she confessed. "You believe me, don't you?"

Across the room, Lord Sinclair was talking and laughing with Miss Freemont in a way that caused a dull ache to form under Damaris's breastbone. "Yes," she said. "I believe you."

Liza's eyes smoldered. "Look at Nicholas *flirting* with that cat. I'm sure that he has taken many females out into the garden—yes, and kissed them, too. But nobody says anything about *his* being in disgrace."

Damaris felt a rush of anger, which was mostly aimed at herself. Aloud she said, "The less said about this, the better. What happened is no one's business."

But, she added grimly to herself, she would make it *her* business to talk to her so-called brother.

Garland took the wind out of Damaris's sails. Next morning early, before any of the others had risen, he met her as she walked in the garden.

"I must humbly beg your pardon for last night's foolishness," he told her. "I have no excuse except that Lady Liza followed me into that room. She looked as pretty as a rosebud. She obviously wanted me to kiss her, and—"

He made a rueful gesture which was also charming, but Damaris was not taken in by the charm. "How could you be so unwise as to be alone with Liza?" she asked sternly. "Why did you even leave the drawing room?"

"I was trying to escape Lady Freemont," Garland explained. He made a wry face. "That woman must know every bad poet in Sussex. Between the attitudes and the wretched verses, I thought I would die of boredom. Finally I managed to escape, and Lizabeth joined me—"

He broke off, and Damaris, whose own conscience was far from clear, spoke in a troubled voice. "This must never happen again. If I have a week of uninterrupted time, I can finish the book. I am going to shut myself into the Blue Room and write. And," she added sternly, "so must you."

Immediately after breakfast, the supposed Winters retired to the Blue Room, and Damaris went to work. She wrote all morning and afternoon, and had a tray sent to the Blue Room at dinnertime. Next day found her hard at it again until Nancy, who brought up a luncheon tray, told her that Lord Sinclair had driven off somewhere in his curricle.

Garland immediately took advantage of his lordship's absence to escape from his confinement in the Blue Room, but Damaris hardly noticed his departure. She had come to a thorny point in the plot.

"Mushrooms," she said aloud. "Oh, plague take the foul things."

She had thought she had all the necessary facts, but now she realized she did not. Perhaps the scene in the garden had erased important details from her mind, for when Damaris began to write the poisoning scene, she found she did not know how many mushrooms Lord Tedell needed to eat, what the mushrooms tasted like, or even their appearance.

There was no help for it. Damaris decided that she needed to talk to Miss Neece again. But when she asked Nancy to summon the earl's barouche, she was told that Liza and Miss Fuffletter had requisitioned it for a drive.

"Happen tha can take the trap, ma'am," Nancy pointed out. "Tha can drive thysen or have one of the grooms drive. It's nobbut a few miles from Neece Place."

Damaris decided to drive herself. She needed the exercise, and after being cooped up in the house so long, it was good to be in the fresh air. It was a pleasant day, with high clouds shot through with tentative sunshine, and the air was mild and fresh. Damaris slowed her horse in order to admire the scenery and noted that the woods were rich with color. There were purple asters, golden aspens, and several colorful mushrooms.

"Toadstools," Damaris exclaimed. "Oh, what splendid luck!"

She could pick some of these mushrooms and take them to Miss Neece, who would tell her their names. Damaris drew rein and was picking a handful of toadstools when she heard a carriage approaching. "Is that you, Miss Winter?" the familiar voice of Miss Fuffletter warbled. "What, pray, are you doing in the woods?"

The earl's barouche had drawn up nearby. Liza, looking dispirited and somewhat cross, was handling the reins, and Miss Fuffletter was seated beside her.

"I have been collecting these," Damaris explained. "For the book, you know."

"I am grateful that they are not for the table," twittered Miss Fuffletter. She shot Damaris an odd, sly look. "They look like deadly *champignons*, to be sure."

"It is research," Damaris repeated patiently. "I am going to see Miss Neece, who knows a great deal about mushrooms. I am hoping she can identify these toadstools for me."

"If you're looking for Miss Neece, she ain't home," Liza said. "We passed her on the road some time back, and she said she was off to Carling."

Damaris regarded the mushrooms she had gathered. If she returned to Pardom, nothing would be accomplished, she thought, whereas if she drove into Carling, she would probably be able to find Miss Neece.

Half an hour later Damaris arrived in town and drove up to the Silver Snail. The common room of the inn was quiet at this time of day, and apart from a man in olive green drab who sat at the far corner of the room, there were no customers.

Near the tap, Mrs. Freddstick stood polishing pewter tankards. Damaris greeted her and asked if she knew where she could find Miss Neece.

Mrs. Freddstick looked thoughtful. "Nah, then, that's 'ard to tell," she boomed. "She were 'ere and had a cuppa in the coffee room, but then she left while I was talking to them rozzers."

Damaris had a vivid memory of the huge Mrs. Freddstick confronting the law. "About the gaming house again?" she hazarded.

"No, miss, that's closed now. But some o' the ugly customers what used to 'ang about Siddons's 'ave taken to 'anging around the Silver Snail."

Mrs. Freddstick's eyes rolled alarmingly, and her mottled countenance grew almost purple with emotion. "This morning one o' those thatch-gallows made improper advances to my maid, Nelly. The poor child 'ad 'ysterics. I told the constable that if I ever catch those slip-gibbets in the Silver Snail again, I will break their wicked 'eads."

Mrs. Freddstick brought her hand down on the bar with crushing force. Damaris made a diplomatic response and then added, "Is there some way that I can reach Miss Neece? I must speak to her as soon as may be."

Mrs. Freddstick said that she would ask her brother, Jack, to find the lady, and Damaris ordered a lemonade, which was served to her in the coffee room. This chamber was set off from the common room by a half-drawn curtain, and as she took a seat by the window, Damaris recalled having luncheon in this room with Mr. Garland when they first came to Sussex.

So much had happened since that day. . . . Damaris sipped her lemonade and stared out of the window, remembering, until she heard footsteps approaching. She looked up hopefully, but instead of Miss Neece, a tall man in a dove gray driving coat came striding through the door. Damaris's eyes widened in consternation as she recognized Lord Sinclair.

Since the night of the Freemonts' party, she had not exchanged two words with him, and encountering him so unexpectedly now gave her an odd feeling in the pit of her stomach. Not wanting to explain what she was doing in Carling, Damaris hoped that he would not see her in the coffee room.

Perhaps he would take a private parlor and so give her the chance to slip out unnoticed? But though Mrs. Freddstick suggested that Lord Sinclair use her best upstairs parlor, his lordship declined. Instead he crossed the common room and sat down next to the man in the olive green coat.

What was he doing here in Carling? Damaris wondered. She watched as his lordship began to talk with the man in green but could not overhear what was being said until Lord Sinclair exclaimed, "Damnation! Are you sure about this?"

"Sure's I'm sitting here, m'lud," his companion replied. "A narsty customer, 'at one. But you knew 'un to be true from the start, like."

"I suspected," Lord Sinclair said, "but I didn't *know*. And what about the woman?"

" 'Er real name is Damaris Cardell."

Damaris felt hot, then cold. She began to feel physically sick as Lord Sinclair said bitterly, "I should have guessed. All that red hair."

Lord Sinclair had set a detective on their trail, and he had discovered her secret. Damaris felt as if she had been slapped in the face. She had heard the disgust in his lordship's voice and could well imagine the expression in his eyes.

Stealthily she got to her feet and backed out of the coffee room and out of the inn. Once outside, she paused to catch her breath. She would drive back to Pardom, she decided, pack her belongings, and leave before Lord Sinclair returned. But before she could find the groom who had taken charge of her horse and trap, a melodious contralto hailed her.

Miss Neece was marching down the road toward her. "Pleasure to see you, Damaris. What? Come into the inn and have some coffee."

"No!" Damaris exclaimed, then hastened to say, "That is to say, thank you, but I am in a hurry."

"But I was told you wanted to see me," Miss Neece protested.

As she spoke, the inn door opened and Lord Sinclair emerged. He stared at Damaris for a moment, and then sketched her an ironic bow. "Your servant, ladies," he said.

The mockery in his lordship's voice left Damaris feeling flayed and exposed. She wished herself a million miles away, but no magic carpet appeared to whisk her to safety, so she faced him and curtsied with as much aplomb as she could muster.

She had nerve, Sinclair thought grimly. He would give her that. But then, to play such games required guts of steel.

"It's fortunate that I met you here, ma'am," he said. "I have several questions to ask you. Will you drive back to Pardom with me now? We can talk on the way."

"But I came in the trap," she protested.

"My tiger will drive it back." Sinclair nodded to his groom, who held his horses' heads.

"Hold on a minute, Nicholas!" Miss Neece exclaimed. She had been watching Damaris's face and felt it time to intervene. "What? Maybe the gel don't want to go with you."

"I think she does, ma'am."

Miss Neece marched up to Damaris and spoke forcefully. "You needn't go anywhere with him unless you want to."

"If she does not," Lord Sinclair said, coldly, "I will conduct our business here on the inn steps."

Damaris guessed that it would give Lord Sinclair great pleasure to make her disgrace public and spoke hastily. "I will go with you, sir."

Sinclair nodded without looking at her. "Miss Neece, your most obedient. Come, Miss—Winter.

It's time you returned to your duties and your devoted brother."

Listening to the sarcasm in his voice, Damaris wished that she could faint and escape the scene to come. But some tattered remnant of courage made her face him and say, "It is not necessary to mock me, sir. I believe that the man in green has told you the truth of the matter."

"So you listen at keyholes, too," Sinclair snapped, and saw her flush and then go paper white. He was almost ashamed of what he had just said, but her lies and deceptions had cut him more deeply than he had thought possible. He felt betrayed and hurt, and wanted to hurt her in turn.

But instead of filling with tears, Damaris's eyes flashed fire. "At least," she retorted, "I did not employ a detective to sneak about!"

How dared she! On the point of delivering a thundering setdown, Sinclair noted that they had acquired an audience. Mrs. Freddstick and her brother were standing on the steps of the Silver Snail and listening avidly. Miss Neece was frowning as she tried to make sense of what was being said.

"I think," Sinclair gritted, "that explanations can wait."

Wordlessly Damaris allowed his lordship to help her into his curricle. Her brief flash of spirit had died, leaving her without comfort or courage, and she remained silent as Lord Sinclair drove out of town.

Finally he broke the heavy silence. "Tell me how you came to hoax my uncle."

Damaris flushed painfully. "I am sorry for that. If the earl had not openly held females in such scorn, I would never have had to lie to him about Desmond Winter. It was wrong of me, but I swear that the earl would not have been the loser. He would have had his book."

Sinclair merely gestured for her to go on and listened in silence as Damaris explained how she had written to the earl and asked leave to come along as her "brother's" secretary.

As he watched her face, Sinclair felt a confused series of emotions. He told himself that nothing Damaris had said excused the lies and the trickery, but at the same time he could not help remembering Cardell House and the family for which she had obviously done these things. He remembered pretty Harriet and Peter's eager, frank face. He recalled the old gentleman's pride and belief in his machine. He remembered grinding poverty endured bravely with a jest and a smile.

Damaris had needed money for all of them, and she had done the best she could. He looked at her searchingly and saw that weeks of living at Pardom had subtly rounded out her face. She was strikingly beautiful, and she had courage. Even now, with her back against the wall, she was not whining or trying to excuse herself. She was facing the music squarely.

Damaris saw him frown and felt a despair that went beyond being unmasked. Lord Sinclair despised her, and she did not blame him.

"It is not Mr. Garland's fault," she said in a low voice. "It was to help us that he undertook this foolish masquerade. I should have known all along that it was hopeless—" She broke off to plead, "He is a kind gentleman, truly. I hope you will not—I pray that you will not blame him."

"Then you don't know who he is?" Sinclair demanded.

Damaris looked puzzled. "Mr. Garland is the grandson of Grandmama's girlhood cose, and—" She broke off to draw a deep breath. "I am telling this badly," she confessed, "but Mr. Garland is not at fault."

"That's all you know." Sinclair's hand closed so tightly on the reins that his grays threw up their heads and snorted. "You obviously know little about the man."

"But I have told you—"

"You didn't suspect, for instance, that he offered to help you only because he was in fear for his life?" Damaris's eyes widened in disbelief. "Ambrose Garland is a thief and a gamester. He has lived by his wits ever since he gambled away the inheritance his parents left him."

Briefly he explained that the detective he had hired, a man called Uxham, had traced Garland's career back several years. The only son of a gentleman of some means, he had apparently served on the peninsula as a lieutenant in a distinguished regiment. But far from covering himself with glory, he had been accused by fellow officers of cheating at cards.

"Nothing could be proven, but there was always a foul odor about him," Sinclair told Damaris. "He left his regiment under a cloud. Later he continued his career in London, squandering away all his inheritance. That was when he began to borrow heavily from a moneylender."

Her eyes had widened with distress. "Do you mean Barnaby White?"

Sinclair's nod was dry. "Cent-per-cents are an unsavory breed, and White is among the worst. According to the detective I hired, White takes real pleasure in hunting down those unfortunates who can't pay their notes. Crimes—none of which could be laid to his door, unfortunately—dog his heels. Apparently Garland owes a great deal to White and needed a place to hide. Pardom must have seemed the answer to his prayers. Even though his enemies tracked him down and know where he is, they haven't dared to come after him there."

It was as though she were watching a puzzle falling into place. "I am persuaded," Damaris mused, "that White was waiting for Mr. Garland at Siddons's. They were sure that he could not stay away from gaming."

Sinclair felt a sudden lift of heart. "Then you truly did not know!" he exclaimed.

She had gone very pale, but she met his eyes steadily. "Did you think me his accomplice in this matter? Of course you would. I cannot ask you to believe me, but I knew nothing of—of his past."

She was speaking the truth. He knew it in his heart, and he felt a rush of joy and relief. Sinclair had no idea why, but it was as though a heavy stone had fallen from his shoulders.

Damaris was too troubled to note the change in Lord Sinclair's expression. "I should never have tried to live a lie," she told him. "I would never have done it except for— But that is neither here nor there. Believe me, I never meant any harm to your uncle or to Liza."

Sinclair's face grew harsh again as he thought of his impressionable cousin in Garland's arms. Damaris might not have intended to hurt anyone, but Garland was another matter.

Damaris was asking. "Must you— Will you tell the authorities?"

If Garland was exposed and sent to prison, what would happen to Damaris? Sinclair's frown was so deep that it cut furrows between his black brows. "It must be my uncle's decision," he said at last, "but I don't think he'll inform the police. Pardom will not want to appear ridiculous." He paused. "I have said nothing to him yet."

"Then will you let me tell him myself?" Though her voice was studiedly emotionless, her eyes pleaded. "I wish only to—to try and explain. And to apologize. If he wishes me to write the book, I will do so without cost to him. If he does not, I will repay the hundred pounds he advanced me. I swear I will."

"I believe you," Sinclair exclaimed.

It was as if the sun had burst through the clouds. The guilt of having lived a lie disappeared in the realization that Lord Sinclair could still trust in her word.

"Thank you," she said, and Sinclair caught his breath at the radiance in her face. The very next moment, she was clawing at him and pushing him backwards, while he fought to control his plunging grays.

"Damnation, woman!" he shouted. "What in the devil's name—"

There was a cracking sound and something whizzed past his cheek. The horses snorted and reared in shock as a bullet slammed into the spot where he had been sitting not a moment ago.

Someone was shooting at them. Shooting to kill.

Chapter Nine

Another shot rang out. Sinclair pushed Damaris down to the floor of the curricle and whipped his grays around a sharp curve in the road. Here he drew rein, dismounted, and tossed her the ribbons.

"Wait here," he ordered. "If you hear another shot, get away. Quickly."

"You cannot be going back—"

But Lord Sinclair had already vanished into the trees that edged the side of the road. Damaris waited until she could bear it no longer. Then, turning the horses, she began to backtrack along the way they had come. Before she had gone far, she heard a rustle of branches, and Lord Sinclair reemerged onto the road.

He climbed back into the curricle and took the reins from her, demanding, "Didn't I tell you to wait?"

"Did you find anyone?" she cried.

"Whoever shot at us is long gone." Sinclair whipped up the horses. "No doubt it was a footpad desperate enough to attack in the daytime. How did you come to see him in time?"

"I saw sunlight flash on metal."

Glancing sideways at Damaris, Sinclair was horrified to see that there was a tear in the right sleeve of her dress. "Good God," he exclaimed, "you're hurt!"

Damaris glanced absently at her arm. "Don't regard it. The bullet merely grazed the skin."

But he halted the horses and examined her arm. The creamy white skin was marred by a scarlet line, and Sinclair's lips tightened. "Good God," he repeated. "You might have been killed."

"Indeed not. I have researched ambushes and know how to deal with them."

"You are talking nonsense," Sinclair said roughly. He unwound his neckcloth and began to bandage Damaris's arm.

"In *A Lady of Mystery* Lord Tedell is ambushed by villains who hide behind the trees. Fortunately, he sees the sun glint on the muzzle of a pistol and foils their plot. The twins helped me by pretending to be the villains and hiding behind the stable," Damaris continued, "and I was Lord Tedell. We used the kettle instead of a pistol, but there was that same flash of light."

She knew she was starting to babble, but she could not seem to help it. As the events of the last fifteen minutes finally sank in, she had begun to tremble. Sinclair put a bracing arm around her shoulders.

"Steady," he said. "It's all right, Madam Mystery."

She looked up at that, but his thoughts were far afield. "If I find who that was," he was saying, "I will kill him."

The arm around her tightened. Damaris knew that she should draw away from his lordship, but she could not bear to forgo his support. His uncompromising strength bolstered her own courage.

"The important thing is that we are unharmed," she said in what she hoped was a cheerful voice. "Edward used to say that a miss was as good as a mile—"

Damaris stopped talking. She had remembered the bullet that had not missed, the one that had ended Edward's young life at Waterloo.

"Edward," Lord Sinclair was repeating. "Your cousin—no, your brother, is it not? Was he truly killed at Waterloo?"

Sick and heartsore, she nodded, and in the bleak silence that followed, she relived all her grief. Mama's death, Papa's suicide, and Edward going off to war. "Don't worry, Dami, I'll turn up safe and sound," he had promised as he hugged her good-bye, but he had not come back.

Damaris looked up at Lord Sinclair and saw that familiar, shadowed look in his eyes. "You also fought at Waterloo," she dared to say. "Will you tell me if it was—was very bad?"

Though he wanted to brush Damaris's question aside, Sinclair found he could not do so. The attempt on their lives had stirred ugly memories, and now they crowded close. He could almost hear men shouting and horses screaming in pain. He could hear and smell the pounding cannons.

Absently Sinclair rubbed his right forearm. The scars for which he had been honored were aching, and his arms felt stiff as if from the endless slash and parry of battle. He could hear John Meere and Archie Smayhaven calling encouragements to each other and to him, and then Monty Graye's cry of pain. "Nicholas," he could hear Monty gasp, "Nicholas—I'm done for. Good-bye, old fellow."

He had fought standing over Monty's body and tried to shield it, fought even when he was wounded and exhausted and fighting on sheer nerve. Finally there had been reinforcements, and he had helped to carry the dead and wounded to the rear. And among the dead had been Monty and Smayhaven and John Meere.

That had been Waterloo, but no woman wanted to hear about such things. Sinclair started to frame a comforting lie and then looked into Damaris's dark eyes.

"Tell me," she urged. "Tell me the truth. I have asked before, but no one will tell me. They say that war is glorious and that Edward died without pain. They lied, did they not?"

"Yes," he replied curtly.

Some of the color ebbed from her cheeks, but her eyes remained steady. "Please tell me," she repeated.

He had intended to bury the war deep within him and never speak or think of it again. But with her eyes on him, he found himself saying, "I went to fight Boney with a jest and a song on my lips. Four of us—friends from schoolboy days—had joined the regiment together, and somehow we got through the peninsula unscathed. We became closer than brothers. And then, at Waterloo—"

He fell silent. After a while she prompted, "At Waterloo. . . ?"

"My friends were killed," Sinclair replied.

Just ahead of them, a yellow butterfly was dancing in the sun. A thrush was singing joyously among the ash leaves, and the cool air was fresh, apple-crisp, flavored with woodsmoke. The homely, ordinary sounds and scents of an English autumn underscored the horror of what Lord Sinclair was telling her.

"I suppose we were young and foolish," Lord Sinclair was saying. "We thought we were prepared for death. But when those fellows were killed and only I survived—" He broke off and after a moment added quietly, "Nothing seemed to make sense—or matter very much—after that."

Damaris wanted to weep for all Edward had suffered, for what Lord Sinclair still suffered. She knew that a part of Nicholas Sinclair had died along with his friends at Waterloo and felt sick with pity for him.

She could think of nothing to say except "Thank you for your honesty. It must have been terrible for you. Too terrible even to remember."

Impulsively she put out a hand to clasp his, and Sinclair was surprised and touched. The thought that Damaris had put aside her own tragedy to give him comfort made him want to do something for her, too, to tell her something that might soften the horror of her brother's death.

"Not everything was terrible," he heard himself say. "There were acts of courage, and simple kindness. Once I saw one of our wounded give the last of his water to a dying French soldier."

Tears brimmed Damaris's eyes. "Thank you for telling me that. It helps somehow to know that—Thank you. I know that Edward would have shared his water with someone. And—and I am glad you came home safely, my lord."

It was almost as though some wound deep within him had begun to heal, for he felt cleansed and renewed. Sinclair looked into Damaris's dark eyes and felt a sudden lightening of his heart. He realized that the day was bright and full of promise and that her hand was light on his arm, and hardly knowing, he gathered her to him and kissed her.

It was as though their lips had found each other after a long loneliness. It was as if nothing and no one else existed—or mattered—in the world. Damaris could hear him whispering her name, and with that sound sweet on his lips, knew that she was in love with Lord Sinclair.

She had been in love with him for a very long time. Just how and when the phenomenon had occurred did not matter. What signified was that Lord Sinclair trusted her even though he knew that she had lied to his uncle.

Damaris did not want to think of the earl, but she could not will herself to forget the ugly things that Lord Sinclair had told her about Ambrose Garland. And she had been the one who brought Garland to Pardom.

When Sinclair felt Damaris stiffen in his arms, his first reaction was to hold her more tightly than before. He could not get enough of her lips or the flower smell of her skin. But when she pushed away from him, the beginnings of conscious thought returned.

What are you doing, you fool? he asked himself.

Not an hour ago he had unmasked Damaris Cardell as a fraud. He still did not know for certain how deeply she was involved with Garland. Yet he had told her the deepest secrets of his heart and now stood kissing her on the open road.

Lord Sinclair loosened his hold on Damaris. She retreated as far as she could in the narrow curricle, and they looked hard and warily at each other. For a moment neither spoke, and then Damaris said, "I—think it is time we returned to Pardom."

Determined though it was, her voice held a wistfulness that caught Sinclair like a blow to the heart. His instinct was to gather her back in his arms and kiss her again, but by now logic and reason were taking control.

Uxham had painted an ugly picture of Damaris Cardell's confederate. Garland was suspected of more than fuzzing cards and palming loaded dice on his comrades. There was the matter of a lieutenant in his regiment, a man to whom Garland had owed considerable sums of money. That young officer had been found dead outside of camp.

The official verdict had been that the lieutenant had been killed by French infiltrators. But, Sinclair thought grimly, an English bullet could kill as easily as a French one.

And once having committed murder, a man might easily be tempted to kill again. . . . Sinclair glanced at the woods that lined the road to Carling, picked up the reins, and urged his grays forward.

After a few moments he spoke formally. "Miss Cardell, I apologize for my actions. It won't happen again."

His voice chilled Damaris and also effectively killed any lunatic ideas she may have harbored. "I beg you will not refine upon it," she replied in what she hoped were equally formal tones. "Such contretemps are not unusual at stressful moments. I recall, in fact, that Lord Tedell once kissed a lady in such an instance."

And a kiss could well be used to divert suspicion. Sinclair frowned at the ugly thought. No, he did not know how deeply Damaris was involved. Desperate to keep her family afloat, she may have turned a blind eye to Garland's tricks.

And that reminded him of another problem. If confronted with his misdeeds, someone like Garland could turn nasty. He did not want trouble, not with Liza in the house, so he would have to choose the moment in which to unmask the man.

Abruptly he said, "I must ask a favor of you. Say nothing about Garland's true identity to my uncle. I have my reasons for wanting the masquerade to continue awhile longer."

When they returned to Pardom, the agitated gateman informed them that the parish constable had been summoned, because "villains and murderers" had been sighted on the premises.

"Big, 'airy villains, they was, my lord," the gatekeeper elaborated. "They was seen a-skulking and a-sneaking around the house, an' it's afeared that money is missing and all. 'Is honor the earl 'as sent for the constable."

Murton confirmed all of this when they reached the house. "Money has been stolen, as well as my lord earl's diamond cuff links and ring," he informed Lord Sinclair in tones of great indignation. "Such a thing has not happened at Pardom in all the years I have served the Family. His lordship the earl has ridden out with the officers of the law."

"Is Mr. Winter with them?" Sinclair asked.

"No, m'lord. He had ridden away to call upon Lady Freemont before the blackguards were sighted. Something about a meeting of the Sussex Muses, I believe."

While Lord Sinclair gave orders that his horse be saddled so that he could join his uncle in the field, Damaris climbed the circular stairs to her room. She wondered if the man or men who had ambushed them were the same ones who had stolen the money and the earl's diamonds. Perhaps—and this made unpleasant sense—the thieving ruffians were Barnaby White and his henchmen, who had finally become brave enough to flush Mr. Garland out of Pardom.

"Oh, what a mare's nest this all is," Damaris groaned.

There was a knock on the door and Liza poked her head into the room. When invited to come in, she plumped down in a chair by the bed and began to complain. "Can you believe it? Lady Freemont has asked Des— I mean, Mr. Winter to her house again. Of course, he went. He is interested in Caroline Freemont."

Damaris conjectured dismally that Liza might be right. If Garland was so desperate for money, he would be looking to marry a plump-pursed heiress. But, she reasoned, the Freemonts were no fools. Lady Freemont might enjoy lionizing a handsome writer who was protégé to an earl, but she would hardly consider that writer as a suitor for her daughter.

Liza continued gloomily, "You understand how I feel, but she— Oh, I *wish* she would go away."

"Miss Freemont?"

"No, my governess. She's been dropping little digs all day about how *ladylike* Miss Freemont is."

Damaris said nothing. She was wondering what would happen when Liza learned that "Desmond Winter" was really an adventurer named Ambrose Garland.

"Fuffletter acts humble and harmless," Liza continued, "but she's a spiteful old bleeter. I've seen her bully servants that can't talk back, and she gives herself airs about her well-connected cousin until I could scream. Of course, she's green-jealous because Papa respects you, and Nicholas likes you."

Damaris felt as if someone had slapped her in the face. "That is fudge," she exclaimed.

"Truly, Damaris, he does. Sometimes he looks at you in *such* a way. I wish," Liza went on plaintively, "that Desmond would look at me like that."

The door creaked open, disclosing a pale-eyed, weak-chinned face. "There you are, my love," Miss Fuffletter fluttered.

"Devil fly off," Liza exclaimed irritably, "why can't you leave me alone?"

"I beg pardon, I am sure, if I have ventured where I am not wanted." Miss Fuffletter sent Damaris a poisonously sweet look and eeled herself into the room. Her elastic body swayed a little as though not quite sure whether to go or stay. Her pale green eyes darted from Liza to Damaris and back again.

"I have been looking for you *everywhere*, my lady," she whined. "In times like this—with scoundrels and dastards lurking behind every bush—it is imperative that we stay together." She flashed a look at Damaris, adding with barely concealed spite, "Of course, if you prefer to remain with Miss Winter, I will *understand*. Her society is far more interesting than my own."

Damaris felt terribly uncomfortable. "Miss Fuffletter is your governess, Liza," she said. "You should go with her."

"Dear Miss Winter. Since *you* say it is so, Lady Lizabeth will listen." The governess twisted her hands together. "Come, Lady Lizabeth, come."

Liza made a face over the governess's head as she was led from the room, but Damaris could not smile back. She was still unnerved by the blaze of hostility she had seen in the governess's eyes.

But it did not signify. She would be soon gone from this house, away from all the lies and deceits and from Lord Sinclair.

The gloomy thought remained with Damaris as the afternoon lengthened. With twilight the earl returned and could be heard stamping and bellowing that, never mind the law, he was going to make sure that no slip-gibbets stole from *him*. Shortly afterwards, candles were lit in the house, and it was time to dress for dinner.

Damaris did not want to go down to dinner and face Lord Sinclair again. She did not want to have to continue lying to the earl. Most of all, she hated the thought of having to watch Garland play his false game, especially since he could be unmasked at any moment. But hiding in her room was not only cowardly, it would only prolong the agony.

Resolutely Damaris descended the circular stairs

and was surprised but immensely relieved to find the earl alone in the drawing room, where a fire burned against the early October chill. He was munching on a large plateful of meat pasties.

"Ah," the earl growled, "there you are. Winter's not here. Must have decided to stay at the Freemonts' for dinner."

Damaris listened patiently while Pardom, in between large bites of pasty, described how he and various constables, footmen, under-footmen, and ground servants had beat the bushes looking for the robbers.

"Bacon-brained, those constables," he fumed. "If Winter had been here, he'd have made short work of it all. Used his brain-box the way Tedell does, d'you see? Didn't flush the curst scoundrels out, so Nicholas went on to Carling to make sure they ain't hiding there. Small consolation that since he ain't back, I can have the whole trayful of these pasties the cook made for him."

Pardom glowered at the last pastry, hesitated, and offered it halfheartedly to Damaris. She was declining when Liza and Miss Fuffletter joined them. The governess shot a sly look at Damaris, archly wondered whether dear Mr. Winter would dine at the Freemonts', and thus caused Liza to subside into gloom.

Since the earl insisted that Lord Sinclair would not expect them to wait on him, they all sat down to dinner at the proper time. The first course was a cressy soup, followed by a dish of pickled eel, glazed sweetbreads, and a quarter of mutton. Liza picked at her food, Damaris had no appetite, and Miss Fuffletter refused the eel, which, she said, gave her spots. The earl ate heartily and became more cheerful.

"Tell me," he said, "has Winter decided how Cuthbert's going to try and scrag Tedell? Said something about mushrooms which I couldn't make out."

Before Damaris could answer, Miss Fuffletter exclaimed, "Mr. Winter had *such* a clever idea, my lord. The wicked Sir Cuthbert is going to poison Lord Tedell."

The earl looked disappointed. "But he did that before in *Knight of the Blood.* Poison was in the port. Not like Winter to dish up last week's stew."

He had aimed his remark at Damaris, but once again it was Miss Fuffletter who exclaimed, "Not poisoned wine, my lord—poison mushrooms. I am not at all clever like Miss Winter—I could *never* do the things she does—so the idea of gathering poisonous mushrooms makes me shiver." Suddenly she swiveled toward Damaris, asking, "What happened to those toadstools you gathered today, ma'am? Did you get the information you wanted from Miss Neece?"

"What in hell are you nattering on about?" the earl growled.

It irritated him to be reminded of Arabella Neece. She was easily the most unsettling female he had ever known, and Pardom glowered into his wine as he remembered how she had humiliated him about his gaming at Siddons's. Perhaps in this she had been right—that young fool Widdersby's shooting himself had made for a bad taste in the mouth—but her opinions about his treatment of Liza were the outside of enough.

Pardom's wattles turned magenta as he recalled what Arabella had said. She had dared intimate that he, Pardom, was afraid to become too fond of Liza for fear he might lose her as he had lost Clara.

It was all curst nonsense, of course. Clara, much as he had cared for her, had been remiss in presenting him with a peagoose of a daughter. As for

Arabella, she did not know her place. He would have nothing more to do with her, and yet—

The earl sighed. It was irrational, but on occasion he actually missed the plaguey female. She did not simper or fuss or defer to him as a female should, but she could hunt, she could shoot, she was a cool hand in trouble. She was as game as a pebble, Arabella, even though he often wanted to strangle her.

Thoughts of Miss Neece had brought a dull ache to the earl's stomach. In fact, he felt positively queasy. "Where's the next course, hey?" he demanded irascibly of a hovering footman. "Ain't got all night, curse it. Must a man starve to death in his own house?"

The second course was a hearty presentation of capons stuffed with apples and walnuts. The earl helped himself liberally and frowned about the table. It was an uncomfortable feeling to be entirely surrounded by females, which probably accounted for his growing queasiness. But, he reminded himself, anyone who had to look at that Fuffletter woman while eating was bound to feel sick.

"But did you not go on to Carling, Miss Winter?" Miss Fuffletter was twittering. "Did Miss Neece tell you about the mushrooms?"

"To hell with you and the mushrooms," the earl snapped.

The governess collapsed like a landed jellyfish, and Liza remarked acidly, "I suppose you are roaring because you want to be rid of us. You want to smoke your filthy cigar and drink your beastly old port."

She flounced up from the table, and the earl watched her go with a baleful eye. Never mind what Arabella had said, the minx was getting above herself. He would pack her off to a young ladies' academy where they would teach her deportment. That would get rid of her tongue *and* the Fufflettter female.

The pleasant thought made the earl smile. Suddenly the smile died from his lips. A spasm of pain had attacked him in the region of the belly. Worse, it seemed as if something was wrong with his eyes. He squinted hard at Miss Winter and saw two of her.

"Curse it," exclaimed the earl. "Can't be disguised. Drank hardly nothing at all."

The ladies stopped at the doorway and Liza exclaimed, "What are you nattering on about, Papa?"

The earl drew out his handkerchief and mopped his suddenly steaming brow. As he did so, the cramp came again. It began in his midsection and then, wavelike, embraced the whole of him.

The earl took a deep breath, tried to rise from the table, and instead fell forward onto the carpet. Miss Fuffletter began to scream. Liza shouted, "Papa," and ran over to him while Damaris tugged the bellpull as hard as she could.

"The earl has been taken ill," she told Murton when he came hurrying in. "Send for the doctor and have his lordship's valet come here at once."

She knew the symptoms of food poisoning, for once Peter had been taken ill after having eaten tainted crab. She remembered the pickled eel that had been served tonight but had no time to refine on it. Instead she helped Yibberly, the earl's frightened valet, make sense of what the earl was saying.

"Belly," he groaned through the terrible cramps. "Going to die."

He was immediately shaken by terrible spasms, and Damaris held his head over the basin that Murton had produced. It had to be the eel, Damaris thought. So far, all the earl's symptoms pointed to food poisoning.

The servants had gathered about the open dining

room door and peered in with frightened faces, and seeing that even Murton was all abroad, Damaris took charge of them all. She sent a footman to fetch the doctor and meanwhile ordered that the earl be carried to his bed and kept warm.

Liza had gone very pale. "Is he dying?" she whimpered.

Damaris shook her head. "I believe the earl to have food poisoning," she said. "It is necessary to absorb and eliminate the toxins in his body, so he must be purged with a saline draft."

Her competent air seemed to convince the butler, who snapped an order that sent a footman racing to the kitchen. Meanwhile Damaris bent over the earl and saw that his eyes were full of tears. "Does it hurt so much?" she cried, distressed.

"Not crying—eyes keep filling up—see two of you" was the slurred answer.

Damaris saw that the earl's pupils had contracted to pinholes. She felt a stab of real panic but said stoutly, "You have had some bad eel, and it has made you sick. We must wash your system clean of the poison."

"Poison," moaned Miss Fuffletter. "It is as I have suspected. It is poison!" She began to have hysterics, and was taken away to her room by one of the footmen.

Liza wanted sincerely to help, but she was so nervous and frightened that she kept dropping things and getting in the way. She seemed relieved when Damaris finally asked her to oversee the boiling of the water in the kitchen.

Damaris herself, with Yibberly's and Murton's help, began to purge the earl, but the symptoms got no better. No matter what they did, the terrible cramps and retching continued. The earl was bathed in sweat, his eyes poured with uncontrollable tears. Not knowing what else she could do, Damaris sat beside him and held his head when he was sick.

Toward midnight, the junior footman sent to fetch the doctor returned alone with the grim news that Dr. Gallin had been called away to attend a difficult birth in Falls-on-Wold, several hours ride away. He would not be home that night.

"Doctor? Doctor?" the earl croaked. "Is the countess having another issue, hey? A son, this time, Clara. Give me a son."

"He is beginning to rave, Miss Winter," Murton said in a low voice. "If only Lord Sinclair were here."

Yibberly began to weep, and Damaris felt like crying, too. Instead she said bracingly, "The earl is a strong man and has everything to live for. I am persuaded that the crisis will pass."

The hours crawled by. Liza came in briefly, burst into tears, and ran out again. Sometimes the earl fell into a feverish sleep. Sometimes he woke, raving and babbling, and had to be forcibly restrained by Murton and Yibberly, who, with Damaris, worked tirelessly to force fluids down the earl's throat.

Watching the tears slide down Yibberly's cheeks, Damaris felt deeply touched. The earl had seemed like such a hard master that she was astonished to see his servants grieving as they did. She did not put the thought into words, but Yibberly seemed to read her mind.

"His lordship has his ways, Miss Winter," he mumbled, "but he is a good master. And a good man. His bark is much worse than his bite, and those of us that know him understand that he's got a soft heart. I have been with him so many years that I can't bear the thought of his—"

He did not need to finish the sentence. Not knowing what to say, Damaris patted the valet's shoulder in silent commiseration.

A gloomy silence enveloped the sickroom, broken only by the earl's labored breathing. Suddenly there was the sound of the front door opening and Lord Sinclair's voice in the hall.

"His lordship," Murton exclaimed joyfully. "Lord Sinclair has returned."

Relieved almost to tears, Damaris hastened to the landing. "Oh," she exclaimed, "I am glad you are here!"

Sinclair looked up and saw Damaris standing at the top of the circular stairs. Her face was framed with an aureole of dark red hair, her eyes were luminous. In that moment, all of his lordship's logic and reasoning took French leave. It seemed as though he were back in darkened, fragrant gardens where nightingales sang.

With some difficulty he realized that she was speaking again. "I am so grateful you have returned, Lord Sinclair," Damaris was saying. "I am so afraid that the earl is going to die."

Chapter Ten

Sinclair took the stairs three at a time and bent over his suffering relative. The poor fellow did look devilish, he thought.

"What has happened here?" he asked, and when Damaris explained, added, "If it's food poisoning, I doubt if even the doctor can do much more than you already have. All we can do is wait."

As if understanding what was being said, the earl groaned, "Don't leave me, woman. . . . Beloved, you can't die and leave me again. Curse it, you can't."

"He is talking to his dead countess," Damaris explained in answer to Sinclair's astonished look. "He has been mistaking me for her all night." She bent closer to the sufferer and took his hand. "I will stay here, so do not be afraid. I won't leave you."

Apparently comforted, Pardom clasped Damaris's hand and fell into a troubled sleep. Yibberly went to stand at the foot of the earl's bed, and Murton hurried away to order restoratives.

Sinclair took a seat near the bed and looked hard

at Damaris. She appeared pale, and there were dark smudges under her eyes.

"You're played out," he exclaimed.

She shook her head. "I will stay with him a little longer," she said. "I am glad you came when you did, sir. He has been asking for you."

Sinclair wished that he had been at Pardom when the earl fell ill, but he had been trying to run Garland to earth. He had first followed the man to the Freemonts' but had found that he had never arrived there.

Abruptly Lord Sinclair got up from his chair, opened the French windows at the end of his uncle's bedchamber, and stepped out onto a small stone balcony. It was cool and still dark, but the birds had scented the dawn and had already begun to racket amongst the trees.

Where Garland was by now was anyone's guess. The loose fish had apparently realized that Barnaby White had lost patience and had come to Pardom to flush him out. Sinclair was almost sure that Garland had stolen the money and the diamonds during the course of his stay at Pardom. These trifles would stand him in good stead now that he was on the run.

Should he have followed his first instinct and turned the law on Garland? The problem was that by unmasking the man, he could also bring scandal down on his relatives—

There was a footstep behind him, and Sinclair turned to see Damaris framed against the open French window. "What is it?" he asked sharply. "Is he worse?"

She shook her head. "He is sleeping more peacefully now. I was truly worried," she confessed. "Peter was ill when he ate that tainted crab, but not nearly as sick as this."

Sinclair was an honest man. He had to recognize

that it was not only for his uncle's sake that he had hesitated to set the law on Garland. It was because of Damaris.

Guilt through association would be enough to bring ruin upon Damaris and her family. Sinclair thought of pretty Hetty and earnest young Peter and the exuberant twins. He thought of Belle nestling against his shoulder and of old Lord Cardell cursing his Wonder.

"No," Sinclair said aloud. "No."

Damaris could not see his face on the dark balcony, but the odd note in his voice worried her. "Do you feel ill, too?" she asked. "You look tired, my lord. Tired and troubled. You should rest before the dawn breaks."

Sinclair looked down at her and thought that it would be incredibly sweet to see Damaris Cardell's face each dawn of his life. Madness, of course.

"First you save my life, then my uncle's," he said aloud. "Pardom is an old curmudgeon, and I could cheerfully wring his neck sometimes, but—"

"It is hard to lose people you love," Damaris finished for him.

In a few short days, a week at the most, Damaris Cardell would be gone from Pardom. He would undoubtedly never see her again. The thought should have brought Sinclair relief, but instead he felt regret as sharp as the thrust of a sword.

He could hardly recognize his voice as his own as he said, "You're right. It's unbearable losing the one you love. Damaris—"

"Hello—hello, the house!"

Both Damaris and Sinclair started. "Good God," he exclaimed, "it's Arabella Neece!"

Damaris could hear Miss Neece's clear voice ascending the stairs. "I brought the doctor," she was proclaiming. "What? Ran him to earth in Upper Selvin', and here we are."

Yibberly leaped to attention as Miss Neece marched into the room. Trailing her was a small, balding man with tufts of hair growing out of his ears. He carried a black bag and looked sleepy but resigned.

Like a conquering general Miss Neece advanced toward the earl's bedside.

"Good thing that the footman you sent to find the doctor met one of my grooms along the way," she exclaimed. "What? Mean to say, I sent my people scurryin' all over the place to pick up the sawbones's scent. What I always say—if you want a job done, do it yourself."

She shot a critical look at Yibberly, who was rubbing sleep from his eyes. "Never thought to see the day *you*'d fall asleep at your post, man." Then, as the valet began to stammer excuses, she interrupted in a different tone, "How bad is he?"

"Much better," Sinclair answered as, followed by Damaris, he reentered the sickroom. "Thanks to this lady's presence of mind and nursing."

Miss Neece favored Damaris with a friendly grin. She then stalked over to the earl, took his wrist, and felt for a pulse. At this, Pardom opened an eye and faltered, "Arabella, that you?"

A look of joy flashed into Miss Neece's intelligent eyes. For a moment her expression softened, and she spoke almost gently. "There you are, then, Molyneux. Thought you was cockin' up your toes."

"Feel sick," the earl moaned. Damaris started toward him but was forestalled by Miss Neece.

"I'll take care of him, now that I'm here. I've known Molyneux Beekley since we was in leadin' strings together, what? Soon have him back on his feet."

The doctor cleared his throat at this. "It might be better," he said tentatively, "if the room were cleared—"

He broke off under Miss Neece's frown and glanced imploringly at Lord Sinclair, who said, "Excellent suggestion. We'll leave Dr. Gallin to make his diagnosis. Yibberly, assist the doctor. Murton, have some coffee brought up."

He caught Damaris's elbow with one hand, grasped Miss Neece's firmly with the other, and propelled them out of the room. "Unhand me, boy," Miss Neece spluttered. "What? Didn't ride all this way at the crack of dawn to stand waitin' in the hall."

"No, but the fact of it is that Liza needs a friendly shoulder to lean on. Miss—Winter is too exhausted to do much more."

Damaris's heart sank as she noted the pause before her assumed name. For a while anxiety over the earl had made her forget what Lord Sinclair must think of her.

She was suddenly very tired and wanted nothing more than to crawl into her bed and sleep. Miss Neece, however, had other ideas.

"Where is the poor gel?" she was asking. "You come with me, Damaris. No, Nicholas, not you. What? Only make the poor child nervous."

They found Liza asleep in a withdrawing room near the earl's chamber. Unable to stay at her father's bedside, she had decided to wait within earshot of the sickroom and had fallen asleep on an uncomfortable horsehair chair. When Damaris bent over her, she started awake and wailed, "Is Papa dead?"

Damaris put her arms around the girl. "No, he is much better. The doctor is with him now."

"And who brought the sawbones?" Miss Neece interjected cheerfully. "What? Molyneux'll be up and makin' himself disagreeable in short order and wishin' us all in Jericho."

Liza giggled nervously, but something in the older woman's voice made Damaris say, "I am persuaded he will not. He was glad to see you a short while back, ma'am, of that I am sure."

"Yes, well." Miss Neece made a dismissive gesture. "When he feels better—"

"When he feels more the thing," Damaris interrupted, "the earl will no doubt feel the need for companionship. Remember, dear ma'am, what you once told me—that a woman of character is not afraid to seize the moment."

Before Miss Neece could reply, there was a knock on the door, and Murton requested that the ladies join the others in the sickroom.

"Lord Sinclair wishes the doctor to address the household," Murton explained. He bowed, hesitated, then added, "If I might make so bold, Miss Winter, it has been a privilege to serve under you tonight. Yibberly feels as I do. We—we both have been in my lord earl's service for many years and are more grateful than words can express that he will be restored to health."

He made a hasty departure and Liza exclaimed, "Well! I have never heard Murton in *that* voice before—nor seen tears in his eyes, neither. You have made An Impression, Damaris."

On the way to the earl's bedchamber, they encountered Miss Fuffletter. That lady's clothes were rumpled, and her hair was untidy, as though she, too, had slept in her clothes. When she saw Liza, she clasped her hands to her bosom, rocked back and forth as though about to faint, and implored Heaven not to punish a poor, innocent maiden by making her an orphan.

The effect of this speech was rather dampened by Miss Neece, who said she had heard it at Astley's Amphitheater. "Don't let Molyneux hear you consignin' him to the tomb," she advised. "What? Not the thing to tell a chap who's feelin' hagged."

She swept in ahead of the others and marched

over to the earl, who was now sitting propped up by several pillows. He looked pale but much more like himself, and a ghost of a scowl formed across his eyebrows when he saw Miss Neece.

"So you *was* here," he growled. "Thought I'd dreamed it. Man can't even be sick in peace without the whole curst county descending on him."

Miss Neece smiled, said, "Rubbish," in no uncertain terms, and sat down in a chair near the bed. Pardom next glowered at the unfortunate governess, began to say something disparaging, then saw Damaris.

He blinked hard, cleared his throat noisily, and began again. "Yes, well. I'm told you sat up with me all night. Curst good of you, ma'am."

Damaris saw Miss Fuffletter glance at her. There was so much jealousy in that pale green gaze that she felt as though she had been slapped. But before she could refine on it, Murton entered the room.

"As you ordered, m'lord," he announced, "the staff has been assembled."

As he spoke, the staff of Pardom Hall filed in. The housekeeper arrived first, followed by the ladies' maids, parlor maid, chambermaids, between maid, scullery maid, and the laundresses. Lord Sinclair's valet took his place beside Yibberly, and the footmen and various under-footmen followed suit. At last came the kitchen staff, consisting of the cook, his assistants, and even the sleepy potboy.

Like a field marshal surveying his troops, Murton flicked his steely glance over the staff. He then turned to incline his head toward Lord Sinclair before retiring to his own place at the apex of the domestic hierarchy.

"What's all this, Molyneux?" Miss Neece boomed. "Should be restin', man, not speechifyin'."

"It's Nicholas's idea."

The earl gestured to Lord Sinclair, who said,

"You've been called here because Dr. Gallin wants to make an announcement."

The doctor cleared his throat and looked both important and grave. "I fear," he said, "that the earl has ingested *Amanita muscaria* or fly agaric. In other words, his lordship has nearly perished from eating poisonous mushrooms."

Dramatically he played up to the ripple of horror which ran through his audience. "The palpitations, the labored breathing, the sweating, salivating, the contraction of the pupils, and the delirium—all these are symptomatic," he intoned. "Fortunately, Miss Winter induced vomiting."

With a cry of "Papa!" Liza flung herself at the earl. He looked astonished, patted her shoulder clumsily, then begged her to take a damper.

"Not in front of the servants, girl," he growled. "Ain't like I'm dying, curse it."

Pale and trembling, Liza retreated to Damaris's side. The doctor continued, "Fortunately, in cases of mushroom poisoning, the victim either dies or recovers in twelve to twenty-four hours. Since the earl has not expired, it is safe to say that he will mend."

At this point the cook burst into tears and swore, by heaven and earth, that he wasn't such a Jack Adams as would mistake a poisoned mushroom from the right kind. "I been picking mushrooms for twenty year without a mistake," he blubbered. "An' I picked those I put into them pies with me own 'ands this morning." "Ask Mr. Winter—'e saw me and spoke to me out in the fields."

"Besides which," Liza pointed out, "we all ate what was served at dinner except for that wretched eel. I don't believe it was mushrooms at all."

"Alas, you are wrong."

The new voice had come from Miss Fuffletter. She had risen from her chair, and her thin body was bent forward like a hound on the scent. "*She* poisoned the earl," she cried, and pointed to Damaris.

Damaris was so astounded that she could only stare, but everyone else had something to say. Pardom suggested that the governess had gone completely mad. Miss Neece begged the patient to be calm, all the while glaring at Miss Fufletter. Liza furiously protested Damaris's complete innocence. Amongst the astounded servants, Nancy could be heard expressing her opinion that Miss Fufletter was a nasty, lying troublemaker.

"Enough," Sinclair roared into the pandemonium. "Be silent, all of you. Ma'am," he added sternly, "you've made a serious accusation. Can you prove it?"

"Of course she can't prove it," Liza retorted. "It's the stupidest, wickedest thing I ever heard. Why should Damaris poison Papa?"

"The fact remains," the doctor interrupted dryly, "that the earl fell ill from eating poisoned mushrooms. It is also a fact that some of the most deadly fungi look like the edible variety. A mistake could easily have been made—"

Miss Fufletter shook her head. "It was no mistake."

"Get that woman out of here," Sinclair exploded. Murton motioned two footmen forward, but the governess eeled past them and ran across the room, where she sank melodramatically to her knees in front of the doctor.

"I saw her gathering poisonous mushrooms. She wanted to learn more about the foul things."

"But—but that was for the book," Damaris stammered. She was so horrified that she could hardly manage to speak coherently. "I had no thought— Indeed, I did not even bring the mushrooms back to Pardom with me."

Sinclair saw that Damaris had gone as pale as

paper and wanted nothing more than to cross the room and put his arms around her. He would gladly have strangled the governess.

Miss Neece exclaimed, "Damaris did ask me about poisonous mushrooms at the Freemonts' party. And again yesterday. What of it? It was all for research."

"No, it was not," Miss Fuffletter panted. "She was the one who inserted the mushrooms into the earl's food."

Pardom frowned. "Just thought of something. There's one thing I ate that nobody else ate—those meat pasties." He broke off to explain, "The cook made them for you, Nicholas, but since you wasn't here, I ate 'em all." Horror thickened his voice. "Remember something else. Offered one to Miss Winter there—she didn't take it."

There was a trace of suspicion in his voice. "*Why* would I wish to harm you?" Damaris pleaded.

"Good question," Miss Neece said at once. "What? No reason Damaris Winter should harm Pardom. He's her brother's patron, mean to say."

"This woman is *not* Miss Winter!" Miss Fuffletter babbled. "I *heard* them talking, she and that so-called brother of hers. Her real name is Cardell, and he is called Garland—Ambrose Garland. They are adventurers and impostors. I am persuaded," the governess went on viciously, "that they came to rob us all."

"Devil fly off!" Liza sprang across the room, caught her governess by the shoulders, and shook her. "How dare you lie about Des— about Mr. Winter! And Damaris didn't run away. She was the one who pulled Papa through!"

"That's right," the earl agreed. "Why should Miss Winter poison me and then stay here to nurse me back to life? Don't make sense. Chuck that curst

Fufffletter out of my room. Can't stand the sight of her."

Again the two footmen stepped forward. Miss Fufffletter looked about her wildly. Her teeth were bared, and in that moment she looked like a hunted animal. Her hope of disgracing Damaris was backfiring, and no one believed her. Realizing that she had cut off her nose to spite her face, she began to cry noisily.

"It is the truth," she wailed. "This woman with the red hair and the black eyes is a thief and a murderess. She and her accomplice have stolen the diamonds and money. She poisoned the earl so as to cause confusion in which they could get safely away."

She squealed as the footmen caught her by the arms, and the desperate sound was too much for Damaris. "Stop this," she cried. "My name *is* Damaris Cardell. But I swear I have never done anything to harm the earl or anyone else."

There was instant and immediate silence. Sinclair leaned down and grasped the staring earl's shoulder. "This is not a matter to discuss in front of the servants," he said urgently.

But for once the earl refused his nephew's counsel. "I want it sorted out here *and* now," he shouted. "I was nearly murdered, curse it, and I want a curst explanation. Now, girl, whatever your real name is, I want the truth!"

Damaris felt as though she were walking a tightrope into a nightmare. She tried to steady her voice as she said, "The man who—who posed as my brother is not Desmond Winter. There is," she added miserably, "no Desmond Winter. It is a pen name I have used because women writers do not get paid as much as men."

The silence that followed was broken by Liza's

despairing wail. "That can't be true. Desmond wouldn't lie to me—"

She was interrupted by a bellow from the earl. "You mean that I was *hoodwinked* by you and that fellow?"

"And she poisoned you, too, my lord," reminded the triumphant Miss Fuffletter. "She should be taken to Newgate. And hanged."

The ground seemed to lurch under Damaris's feet. She turned to Lord Sinclair, pleading, "Surely, *surely* you cannot believe that I would try to harm anyone?"

She could not have attempted murder. He was sure of that. But Sinclair was becoming rapidly convinced that the poisoned pasties had not been meant for the earl.

Learning about Uxham, Garland had intended to stop Sinclair from going to his uncle with the damning evidence. And like a true gamester, he had hedged his bets by making two attempts on Sinclair's life.

Garland knew that Sinclair enjoyed meat pasties. He had learned about poisonous mushrooms from Damaris. It would have been easy to slip such a mushroom into the cook's basket as they spoke together in the field. And then, using the Freemonts as an excuse, he had ridden away to ambush Sinclair on the Carling road.

Only, the ambush had failed and Garland had ridden back to Pardom in all haste. That was when he must have caught sight of White and his henchmen, discovered the game was up, and taken to his heels.

The earl was bellowing, "Tried to take *me* in, did you? Well, my girl, you've met your match this time. Murton, go get the parish constable."

"You'll do nothing of the kind," Sinclair interrupted. "I don't believe for a moment that this woman poisoned you, then turned about and saved your life. And masquerading as a writer's sister is no crime."

He turned to the gaping cook. "At what time did you make the meat pasties?"

"At three o'clock, m'lord," the man quavered. "Put them into the oven meself. You can ask—"

"At three o'clock this lady and I were still in Carling," Sinclair interrupted in the same stern voice. "Miss Neece can vouch for that."

"Indeed I can," Miss Neece said stoutly. "If you think Damaris poisoned you, you're caper-witted, Molyneux. Must've been an accident. What? These things happen."

The earl considered this. "So she didn't poison me," he admitted grudgingly. "Even so, I want her gone. I don't want a curst liar in my house."

"I doubt whether Miss Cardell will trouble you again."

Torn by his various emotions, Sinclair spoke curtly, and the harsh note lacerated Damaris's already aching heart. She forced herself to meet his eyes and could read nothing but disgust in his face.

Of all the things that had been said and done tonight, Damaris thought, that look was the hardest for her to bear.

Nancy helped Damaris pack her belongings. It took some time, because the abigail was upset and angry and kept having to fold and refold Damaris's few clothes.

"It's not right, ma'am, and so I tell thee," she exclaimed through angry tears. "Tha did nothing to nobody, I'll take my oath on it." She paused and added passionately, "It's that Fuffletter. I'd like to take my broom to her."

Damaris knew that Nancy's championship should have made her feel better. Instead, she felt numb.

"Miss Fufflетter felt that I was a threat to her. She thought that I was going to usurp her position and that she would be dismissed. At least," she added in an attempt to console both Nancy and herself, "I am going home."

Nancy muttered under her breath. To her mind, Miss Winter—Miss Cardell, she was now—had been unjustly condemned. The staff, who had all witnessed her courage and determination to save the earl's life, concurred. Yibberly actually shed tears as he wished her farewell. More restrained but as unhappy as the earl's valet, Murton summoned a hackney carriage for Damaris, warned the driver to drive safely, then stood outside in the chill gray drizzle to see her off as though she were Quality.

The gesture touched Damaris, but it did not console her as the hard, rain-washed stone of Pardom Hall retreated into the distance. She wrapped herself further into her cloak and shivered, for the carriage was cold, the cracked leather upholstery felt damp, and her heart felt like a raw wound.

In vain, Damaris tried to think of the future. She would have to pay the earl back his advance, somehow. Perhaps her publishers might take a revised version of *The Heir of Brandon Manor*, she thought, but the way she felt now, she never wanted to think of Lord Tedell again.

Much as she longed for home, she dreaded the explanations that must result at her unexpected homecoming. But when the hired hackney reached Cardell House shortly after sunset, it was at once evident that something momentous had happened.

Every window of the house was bright with candles, and the front garden was cluttered with abandoned toys. Perhaps Peter had been hurt. Or Lord Cardell had done something horrible with one of his inventions—

Damaris jumped down from the hackney and ran

up to the house, reaching it just as Hepzibah threw open the door, and Damaris's jaw slackened at sight of the servant. For the first time since she had come to work for the Cardells, Hepzibah was smiling broadly.

"Is that you, Dami?" Peter came skimming down the stairs to mash his sister in a rib-cracking hug. "You got my wafer, then. Isn't it famous?"

"I do not know what you mean," Damaris was beginning, when all hell broke loose. There was a horrible noise consisting of bells, buzzers, screechers, and clangers, followed by a triumphant howl from Lancelot.

"Grandpapa has sold the rights to his burglar trap," Peter shouted through the bedlam. "An investor is giving us five hundred pounds outright and a percentage of future sales, so Grandpapa is improving on the model."

Just then Lord Cardell appeared at a side door. He was beaming from ear to ear. "Damaris," he yodeled. "Glad to see you, my girl. Heard about my triumph? 'Struth! Long overdue."

Harriet now came running downstairs, followed by Fiona and Lancelot and little Belle. Hugged, kissed, and welcomed, Damaris felt her heartache ease. She was back with her family, back where she belonged.

In the days that followed, she tried to put the past behind her. Spilled milk could never be restored, she told herself, and what had happened at Pardom was best forgotten. Unwilling even to remember that terrible scene in the earl's bedroom, she did not tell her family what had caused her to come home. She did not even tell them about Garland's perfidy. She simply said that she had grown tired of living a lie and had decided to make a clean breast of it. She then added that they owed the earl a hundred pounds.

Lord Cardell paid the money out of his profits. He had an uneasy notion that his eldest grandchild was hiding something, for though she smiled often and made light of her days in the earl's household, there were shadows in her eyes that he did not like. And he noted that whenever Ambrose Garland or Lord Sinclair was mentioned, she changed the subject.

One of those two had hurt Damaris—hurt her badly. Lord Cardell was a man of science, so he set himself to prove his theory by casually introducing first one man's name and then the other's into the conversation.

But his hopes that his granddaughter would betray herself did not bear fruit. Try what he would, Damaris hid behind her smile. "Which means," the old gentleman growled to himself, "they both could have hurt her. A pox on 'em."

Lord Cardell wished that he could confide his fears to his wife, but since his change of fortune, Lady Cardell had been too busy playing the grande dame to worry about anyone else. She spoke of Harriet's "come-out party" in a few years and of ordering gowns from Bond Street couturiers. Such talk made Lord Cardell's blood run cold, and he avoided his wife as much as possible.

Damaris, also, avoided Lady Cardell if she could. It was not her grandmother's posturing that bothered her as much as her frequent mention of Ambrose Garland. The man had made an impression on the old lady, and whenever she could, she asked questions about him in a sly and knowing way. *She thinks I have a tendre for him,* Damaris thought. She wondered what Lady Cardell would say if she knew the truth.

Damaris tried to lose herself in her work. Ironically, in that direction she had succeeded beyond her wildest hopes. Shortly after her return to Kent, she received a letter from Messrs. Dane and Palchard offering her a substantial increase in pay. Knowing that Pardom had approached her to write a book for him, the publishers recognized a potential money-maker. The fact that Pardom had reneged on his offer did not matter. People would read the latest Desmond Winter book out of curiosity.

So Damaris hauled out her manuscript and began to rewrite it. At first she was glad to plunge into work, but pleasure soon changed to pain. One afternoon as she revised the chapter about the prizefight, changing names and altering locations, she found that she could not describe the scene without thinking of Lord Sinclair.

Try as she might, she could not shut out memories of his lordship. She remembered vividly how he had rescued her from those fops and called her "Madame Mystery" for the first time. She recalled his smile and the strength of his arm and how it had felt to be pressed against his lean, hard side as they sheltered from the rain together. Nicholas Sinclair seemed so real, so near to her, that if she closed her eyes, she could feel him, draw in his scent, feel his lips on hers—

"Miss Damaris?"

Hepzibah, her gaunt face screwed up into an expression of greatest melancholy, was standing in the doorway. "Her leddyship wants ter know if you can come down to the morning room," she sighed. "She's got a visitor."

Since the old gentleman's inventions had begun to make money, the Cardells had commenced to move up in the world. Seeing this, the local gentry had resumed calling at Cardell House. The inventor thumbed his nose at those who had ignored them during the troubled years, but the dowager was in her element and received her visitors as though she were the queen of England.

Damaris began to say that she could not leave her work and then recalled the unwanted effect that her work was having on her. Perhaps an hour of making small talk was the antidote she needed.

Wiping the ink from her fingers, she followed Hepzibah to the morning room, where Harriet was helping Lady Cardell entertain her guest. This stylish, sprightly old lady was introduced as Mrs. Glencoe.

"Cleone and I are old friends," Lady Cardell announced grandly. "You do not guess who she is?"

When Damaris shook her head, her grandmother's eye sparkled. "Cleone is dear Ambrose's grandmother," she exclaimed triumphantly. "She was passing through Kent on her way to Bath and decided to stop and see me."

"I see" was all Damaris could think of to say.

"My grandson is a handsome cub," said Mrs. Glencoe complacently, "but he is also something of a rogue. I must say, Miss Cardell, when I heard of you, I hoped."

"Hoped, ma'am?"

"That he would settle down." Mrs. Glencoe smiled as though conferring an untold honor on Damaris. "Like many young bucks, he has sowed more than his share of oats. I have told him many times that it is time for him to marry a suitable female and start his nursery, but so far he has ignored my advice."

Feeling very uncomfortable, Damaris said that she must return to her book. "Lord Tedell's adventures," Lady Cardell explained grandly to her guest. "My granddaughter amuses herself with such romances."

"How quaint. Lucinda, it is in truth romantic that Ambrose has at last been struck by Cupid's dart."

Damaris, who had been halfway to the door,

checked herself and listened as Mrs. Glencoe started to tell the story about her grandson falling in love.

"He will not tell me her name, but he has been writing these past weeks to a lady in Sussex. Perhaps, Miss Cardell, you could help me to discover the identity of the Unknown Fair?"

Damaris thought, wryly, that whatever lady had caught Ambrose Garland's attention must be an heiress. Only a wealthy woman would pay his gaming debts.

"Do you really know nothing of the gel?" Lady Cardell was asking. Her friend hesitated. "Come, come, I insist that you tell me all."

"All I know is that she resides in Sussex and that they have set a place to meet. There was a letter. . . ." She paused. "Of course, Lucinda, you cannot think that I would stoop to read Ambrose's letter."

"Oh, *no*, Cleone. What did it say?"

"The letter was lying open on the desk, and I mistook it for another document. It was quite by accident that I read the words 'Friday' and 'the Silver Snail.' The gel's name, I do not know, but her initials are 'L.B.' "

Damaris started as though she had been stung. "*What* did you say, ma'am?"

"She must be quite a beauty," Garland's grandmother said proudly. "I cannot but mislike this secrecy, but—heigh, ho—the world has changed since I was a gel."

Damaris did not hear her. She had no doubt of it at all that "L.B." was Liza. Garland had somehow contacted her and wormed his way back into her good graces. Now he was going to meet her and no doubt try to persuade her to fly with him across the border.

Damaris clenched her hands into fists. In spite of

his lies, Liza must still fancy herself in love with Garland. The little goosecap would no doubt agree to do whatever he said. And once in his power, she would be ruined forever.

Chapter Eleven

Ambrose Garland consulted his pocket watch. The smart silver timepiece, a recent gift from his doting grandmother, told him that it was half past six in the evening.

She was two hours late. Moodily he took a pull from the flagon of ale at his elbow. At this rate, they would have to travel through the night. It was not the scenario he had envisioned, and it both irritated and worried him.

If Liza did not appear as he had been sure she would, he would be in a devil of a stew. He had played and been played until there was no game left. Debts were owed everywhere. The money he had managed to filch from Pardom before his hasty departure was long gone, and he had used the earl's diamonds to stake one unsuccessful night of gaming.

Garland had heard enough about the events at Pardom to know that he dared not show his face publicly for fear that he might be recognized. Even if Sinclair had not set the law on his heels by now,

White and his hounds would surely be hot on the trail. . . . Garland frowned into the fire of the private parlor that he had bespoken.

That parlor and the table set for two had cost a great deal of money, which he had "borrowed" from his grandmother Glencoe. Unfortunately, it being some sort of market day at Carling, all that he could manage at the Silver Snail was the landlady's personal parlor. It was a fusty, fussy room which smelled of beeswax and heliotrope, but it would have to do.

Garland corrected himself. There was nothing else *to* do. He had tried going to earth at his grandmother Glencoe's, but he could not stay with the old trout forever. With her affectations and peculiarities and her insistence that he dance attendance on her, she drove him half mad. Now he had decided to risk everything in a single throw of the dice.

Once more, Garland pulled out his pocket watch and looked at the time. Seven o'clock. Perhaps Liza had been prevented from coming? The thought made his blood run cold.

He had laid the groundwork almost unknowingly while at Pardom. At the time he had intended nothing more than a mild flirtation, something to amuse himself in that suffocating place. He had overplayed his hand by kissing Liza at the Freemonts' and had cursed himself for falling afoul of Sinclair, but now he blessed the fates that had caused Lizabeth Beekley to fall head over heels in love with him.

How eagerly she had responded to his humble letter, smuggled to her secretly and at great expense. How easily she believed his explanation that he had only wanted to help poor Miss Cardell and her impoverished family. Garland smiled sardonically as he considered how Lady Lizabeth would run, screaming, from him if she knew what he was capable of doing, had, in fact, done in his life. But she did not know, and she had replied to his passionate declarations of love by telling him that she had given him all her heart and that she would never love another.

And then he had suggested that there was *one* way they could be together, but he could not ask it of her because he loved her too much—after which she had been like putty in his hands.

There was a clatter of wheels in the courtyard. Garland sprang to his feet. From the window he could see a hired chaise had drawn up to the inn door. The driver was setting down the steps, and there, in a cloak of dark satin trimmed with swansdown and a bonnet that was swathed with a heavy veil, was Liza.

With an exclamation of relief, Garland left the parlor and ran down the stairs to meet her. The common room of the inn was crowded with farmers, sheepmen, and other rustics, but Garland thrust through the throng determinedly. By the time Liza was ready to descend from the carriage, he was there, hands outstretched.

"My angel," Ambrose Garland exclaimed. "My beautiful goddess."

Liza's heart melted at the sound of his voice. She had been having misgivings all day. When she had consented to fly over the border with him, she had acted in a rush of romantic fervor. Later, reality had set in and she had doubts, then second thoughts, and finally a hen-hearted inkling that she should not go to meet Ambrose at the Silver Snail at all.

"I thought you were not coming," he said, smiling down at her. "I thought you had changed your mind."

He was so handsome, and he spoke so lovingly that the last of her doubts melted away. Liza felt afire with delicious power. "What would you have done if I had not come?" she teased.

"I would have cut my throat," he told her. *Or*, he amended silently, *someone would have cut it for me.* But now that she was here, all would be well. Even if things did not go as he planned and Pardom was not forthcoming with a settlement to rid himself of scandal and an unwanted suitor, he would enjoy initiating Liza in the arts of love.

Garland's smile broadened. Everything was going according to plan.

The horses that pulled the hansom plodded along at a snail's pace, and Damaris chafed at the delay.

Her first reaction to Mrs. Glencoe's revelation was that the earl should be warned, but this presented a problem. She wanted her warning to reach the earl and not anyone else. The less people knew, the better it would be for Liza.

Accordingly, Damaris asked Peter to carry a hastily written letter to Pardom but did not tell him anything beyond the fact that her message to the earl was urgent. She hoped that he would not ask questions, but Peter had grown up a great deal during the past few months.

"Does this have something to do with Garland?" he demanded shrewdly, and when Damaris asked him what made him say such a thing, he explained somewhat impatiently that he was not as cockle-brained as she imagined. "Mrs. Glencoe is Garland's grandmother, ain't she? And it was after you talked to *her* that you came out looking so white. What's in the wind, Dami?"

"I cannot tell you. It is not my secret to tell," Damaris said distractedly. "But if what I believe is true, the earl *must* get this letter."

Peter frowned at the letter in his hand. "Supposing I can't find the earl? He may not be at home."

"Then you must find Lord Sinclair." Damaris did not like the dull ache that still accompanied mention of his lordship. "His estate is in Hampshire, and Murton will send a servant to guide you there."

Peter started to leave the room, then came back. "Don't tell me if you don't want to," he said awkwardly, "but something happened between you and Lord Sinclair. After you came back from Pardom, you've . . . changed."

Damaris felt her cheeks grow hot. She began to deny it, but then she remembered that she had done with lies and deceptions.

"No," she said at last. "Nothing happened that signifies. Peter, we must hurry now—all depends on haste."

With this, Damaris went upstairs to gather up her traveling cloak, her reticule, and a few sovereigns that she had kept back from her publisher's last payment in order to buy Fiona a new winter coat. Then she had Bowens drive her into town; here she hoped to catch the mail coach but, finding that the earliest coach would come in the morning, cast economy to the winds and hired a hansom.

But the horses were incredibly slow, and the driver, a portly individual with a bulbous nose, did not bestir himself in spite of her pleas and even in the face of threats.

"Them 'orses is going as farst as they goes," he replied stolidly when she complained. "They is pulling us, leddy, not the other way around, so we'st do as they wants."

It was sunset when they reached Turnbridge Wells in Sussex, and much later than that when they finally made Carling. Damaris was in agony, sure that by now Garland had met Liza and gone on with her. When she thought of how Garland had used lies and deceit to insinuate himself into Liza's good graces, she felt such rage that she could hardly bear the thought of him. She prayed that Peter had already reached the earl and that Pardom would have the sense to bring retainers and swift horses with which to mount a pursuit to the border.

Finally they reached the Silver Snail. Business seemed unusually brisk even at this late hour, for the inn courtyard was crowded with traps, carts, and horses. Ordering the driver to wait, Damaris descended and hurried into the inn.

The common room was full of laughing, singing, drinking men. Damaris looked about her for the landlady and instead saw her portly brother, Jack, working the pump. "Where is Mrs. Freddstick?" Damaris asked.

Jack looked aggrieved. "M'sister's got the grippe, mum," he sighed.

"I am sorry to hear it," Damaris said. "But perhaps you can tell me—"

" 'Ealthy has a 'orse, the woman is," Jack continued dismally, "and now she's sick on the very week when them sheepmen is 'aving their market. The farmers is coming up to buy the wool and trade their goods, and the inn is chock-full an' all. There's no room to be found anywhere, mum, in case you wants one."

"I do not want a room," Damaris said hastily, "but I do require that—"

"An' there ain't no private parlors neither," Jack interrupted. "Now, if you was to say supper, I could sit you down to a saddle o' mutton an' steak-an'-kidney pie in the coffee room."

Damaris said that she wanted neither a room nor supper. "I am looking for my—my brother."

A gleam of intelligence stirred in Jack's pudding-like countenance. "Ar," he said.

"You have seen him then?" Damaris cried. "Is he here?"

Jack scratched his nose with a beefy finger. "That's as may be, miss."

If he was intent on a romp across the border, the loose fish would have bribed Jack to keep silence. The landlady of the Silver Snail would never have stood for such goings-on, but she was in her sickbed and out of the way.

"I am persuaded," Damaris said carefully, "that my brother wishes no one to know that he is meeting a young lady here. Her relations are wicked and mercenary and do not look with favor on his suit."

It was an excuse she had used in her book *A Lady of Mystery*, and it seemed to work. "Ar," Jack said again. "I saw 'er coming off a hackney." He lowered his tone to add, " 'Er face was veiled, but I could see she was as fine as five pence."

Damaris's heart had begun to pound with both triumph and apprehension. "Where are they now?"

Jack hesitated, then relented. "Seeing as you're his sister, wot's the harm? There wasn't no room anywhere, so I give 'em Maria's sitting parlor on the second floor. End of the hall."

A farmer bellowed, at this point, that it was a sorry thing when an honest man had to wait ten minutes for his pint while the landlord spent his time gossiping. Jack hastily went back to work, and Damaris made for the stairs.

As Jack had said, Mrs. Freddstick's parlor was tucked away at the far end of the corridor. Damaris stood by the closed door for a moment and heard a murmur of voices from within. She knew that Garland was capable of ugly behavior, and for a moment she hesitated. Should she not tell Jack, at least, or seek reinforcement before confronting the jackal in his den?

But Damaris knew that she could not do it. Once word leaked out that Liza had agreed to run off with Garland, tongues would wag all over the country that Pardom's daughter had the morals of a straw damsel.

Damaris drew a deep breath and knocked on the door. Instantly the murmurous voices within fell silent. Damaris knocked again. "Liza," she called softly. "Liza, are you in there? It is Damaris."

There was the sound of a chair being pushed back, Liza's voice raised in a question, and a man's deeper tones. Then the door to the parlor squeaked open, and Liza peered out.

"What are you doing here?" Liza demanded.

She was dressed for travel, Damaris noted. She also saw that the girl's face was tight with apprehension as Liza continued, "Is there— Did anyone come with you?"

Damaris glanced at Garland. He was standing with one booted foot on the andirons of the grate. "I am alone—for the moment."

"Meaning that others will follow," Garland said. His voice, like his face, gave nothing away, but inwardly he was seething. The last person he had expected or wanted to see was Damaris Cardell. He had no idea how the woman had discovered his plans, but he was sure she had come to stop Liza from running away with him.

Garland's lips tightened. If that was the case, he felt sorry for Miss Cardell.

Damaris said, "Your grandmother, Mrs. Glencoe, let slip that you were meeting a young lady at the Silver Snail. I guessed the rest."

"Like your fictional hero, Lord Tedell, you gather facts from clues." His smile was forced. "Come and warm yourself, Miss Cardell. We are about to leave, but it would be a shame to waste this fine fire."

"I thank you, no." She was tempted to accuse Garland to his head but knew that if she denounced

Garland as being the swine he was, Liza might very well become defensive and go off with him.

Damaris looked about the room, which was fussily furnished with overstuffed chairs covered in pink chintz. Potted plants vied with knickknacks on a jardiniere. A hand-stitched sampler claimed that home was the sweetest place in the world.

One of the sofas was set with its back to the door. Damaris sat down determinedly on this sofa and regarded Liza gravely. "I wonder if you know what you are about," she began.

"Of course I do," Liza retorted. "Ambrose and I are running away together."

"Are you?"

"It's the only way, Damaris. Papa would never give his consent to our marriage. And do not treat me as if I were a child," Liza added defensively. "I am a woman."

Garland interjected smoothly, "You are the only woman for me, my angel."

"But until you are of age, you cannot hope for any money of your own," Damaris pointed out practically. "How will you live?"

Liza shrugged. "Money is not important."

"Then this flight across the border is for love and only for love?"

Liza frowned. She had just remembered that it was because of Damaris's lies that dear Ambrose was in disgrace. "What if it is?" she snapped. "What business is it of yours?"

Damaris looked hard at Garland, who met her eyes boldly. "Come, 'sister' Damaris. Wish us happy."

If she could keep them talking, perhaps Pardom would catch up to them. Repressing a strong desire to box Garland's ears, Damaris said, "Liza, I am persuaded that you hold me in dislike. You no doubt believe all that Miss Fuffletter said about me—"

"Oh, *her*," Liza exclaimed disdainfully. "She's gone, and good riddance. Papa said he didn't want sneaks and eavesdroppers around him, and sent her packing. I hear she went off to Worcester to live with Lady Cordelia Armstrother." She paused. "But you were wrong to involve Ambrose in your schemes, Damaris. You knew what a kind heart he has, and you took advantage of him and caused him so much heartache."

"Indeed," Damaris murmured. "Pray tell me more about his—heartaches."

Garland interrupted at this point. "What is there to tell? I went away, knowing that the earl would not allow me to pay my addresses to Liza. But I could not forget her, and I finally wrote to her telling her what was in my heart. She responded."

He smiled down lovingly at Liza, who murmured, "I told him that I loved him and that I wanted to be with him. Ambrose did not want to fly across the border. It was I who suggested it."

But the idea had no doubt been planted carefully by Garland, who was saying, "It is time to go. The horses will be cold, my goddess."

There was no more time. Damaris decided to risk all on one throw of the dice. "Liza," she said, "I do wish you will be happy. But I wonder if you will never miss Pardom. I think you are brave for giving it all up."

Liza, who had been about to reach for her cloak, hesitated.

"Once you go to Gretna Green with this man, you will never again be received at Pardom," Damaris continued earnestly. "Or at Neece Place or—or anywhere else, for that matter."

"It doesn't matter," Liza said sternly, but Damaris saw her eyes darken with that sad, yearning expression with which she had sometimes looked at her father. "Papa won't care anyway. No doubt he'll be glad to be shut of me. And—And Ambrose loves me."

"Indeed I do." Garland put an arm around Liza's waist and drew her close to him.

"And Lord Sinclair?" Damaris prodded. "What will he think of you, Liza?"

At mention of Sinclair, Garland's handsome face hardened. He had nothing but contempt for the earl, whom he considered a caper-witted fool, but Sinclair was another matter.

"We must go, my angel," he said. "Don't listen to Miss Cardell. She's being the dog in the manger."

Damaris noted that under his smile, Garland was nervous. "Lord Sinclair," she prodded, "will not let the matter rest here. He loves you, Liza."

Liza's lower lip trembled, but she rallied. "Nicholas is a bully and I hate him. And anyway, you're wrong. He doesn't care tuppence for me."

"But he does care about the family name," Damaris murmured, and saw Garland wince.

Garland was thinking that Damaris Cardell was undoubtedly right. Sinclair would follow him to the ends of the earth if need be in order to satisfy his sense of family honor. But it would avail him nothing, for by the time his lordship caught up to them, Liza would be hopelessly compromised.

"What we feel for each other is greater than family or life or honor." With a dramatic gesture, Garland threw Liza's cloak around her shoulders and picked up his own coat. "I care nothing for the world or what it may say about us."

Damaris placed herself between the lovers and the door. "That is probably the first thing you have said tonight that is true, Mr. Garland. You really do care nothing for what the world will say about Liza. You are only thinking of yourself, as always."

An ugly look leaped into Garland's eyes. "And

you, Miss Cardell, are lying through your teeth—as always."

In spite of her determination to stay calm, Damaris felt a rush of anger. "At least I do not have gaming debts to hide," she retorted, "nor have I ever stolen from my friends."

"What is she talking about?" Liza wondered.

"Nothing that need concern you, my angel." Garland's handsome face was hard with anger. "Miss Cardell, either you remain quiet, or—"

"Or what?" Damaris demanded. "Will you use force to silence me? Then Liza will see you as you truly are."

Garland strode across the room toward Damaris, who dodged him and got behind the sofa. "Now, madam," he said roughly, "you have exhausted my patience. You will stay here in this room and say nothing until we are on our way, or you'll regret it."

Liza looked at Damaris and then at her sweetheart. "But, Ambrose," she began uncertainly.

"I will not be silent," Damaris interrupted. "I will scream for help, and Jack will send for the watch."

"That you will not, you harpy." Tearing off his neckcloth, Garland lunged at Damaris, who once more evaded him. "I'll tie and gag you."

"But—but you cannot gag and tie Damaris," Liza wailed.

"Believe me," Damaris cried, "he has done a great many worse things. Do you know, Liza, that he is a gamester who is in so deep to the moneylenders that he lives in fear of them?"

"You lie, you witch," Garland shouted.

"He needs money all the time. I am convinced that it was he who the money and diamonds from Pardom, and now he is going to use you to extort money from the earl. Look at his face and tell me if I am right!"

Garland's lips had gone white. Liza gasped, "That is a monstrous thing to say."

"Not more monstrous than what he intends for you," Damaris said desperately. "Think a moment. You will not reach your majority for years. You have no fortune—nothing that will tempt a man like Mr. Garland to marry you."

"Devil fly off, we are running off together because we *love* each other." Liza was nearly in tears.

"He loves your money, not you. He thinks that if he compromises you, the earl will pay a great sum of money to hush up the scandal," Damaris said.

A look at Garland's face told her she was right. "It is a trick employed by unscrupulous men," she went on. "In *A Lady of Mystery*, Lord Tedell's cousin is nearly ruined by a thoroughly Bad Man. The duke, her father, has to pay two thousand pounds to keep Sir Wilkinset from revealing that he had spent a night alone with Lady Frances, and—oh!"

Garland had managed to grasp her arm. "Will you be silenced, bitch?"

His fingers were like steel talons digging into her flesh. Damaris's gasp of pain was drowned out by Liza's protesting wail. "Ambrose, stop—you are frightening me."

He ignored her. "If you know what's good for you, hold your tongue," he hissed at Damaris.

Instead of fear, she felt a wave of loathing. "And if I do not?" she snapped back at him. "Will you try and murder me as you tried to murder Lord Sinclair? It was you, was it not, who shot at us from the woods near Carling?"

It was a stab in the dark. Damaris had the dubious satisfaction of knowing that she was right, for Garland's eyes blazed, then narrowed and became murderous. He snarled, "Be quiet," and slapped her hard across the mouth.

"Then . . . it is true?"

Liza's shocked whisper broke the silence that had followed the blow. Garland turned to her, and his face was hard with anger. "Believe what you want to," he snapped at her, "but you're leaving with me, now. Pardom will spend more than two thousand pounds if he wants his child back."

If he had expected Liza to burst into tears, he was mistaken. After staring at him for a moment, she let out a banshee shriek and leaped at him, beating at him with her fists. Distracted, he fractionally loosened his hold on Damaris, who kicked him as hard as she could. Her toe connected with his shin, and he let out a yell and let her go.

Without pausing to think, Damaris reached down, seized a warming pan, and hit Garland on the back of the head. He fell as if he had been pole-axed.

There was a burst of laughter from the common room below. The farmers and sheepmen were beginning to enjoy themselves in good earnest. In the suddenly silent sitting room, the two women stared at each other.

"Devil fly off," Liza gasped, "that was a wisty castor, as Nicholas would have said." Her face suddenly crumpled. "Oh, Damaris, what a *ninnyhammer* I've been."

Damaris did not waste time trying to console Liza. "Quickly," she cried, "hand me his neckcloth. We had better tie him while we get away."

Liza did not budge. She was looking with loathing down at the man at her feet. "I cannot believe that he would— Oh, Damaris! he told me that I was the queen of his heart. He said that he burned with a pure fire for my love."

"There was nothing pure about him," Damaris

said grimly. "The neckcloth, Liza, please. We will leave Mr. Garland here for the earl to deal with."

"Papa?" Liza looked suddenly scared. "You did not tell him that I— Oh, Damaris, I don't want to face Papa now."

Damaris was thinking much the same thing. "It is best that you get back to Pardom at once," she was beginning when footsteps were heard on the stairs.

Liza turned chalk-pale. "It's Papa. I'm going to faint."

Damaris felt a hen-hearted desire to faint also. Instead, she spoke bracingly. "Fudge," she said. "He cannot eat us. And since I have been here to play chaperon, no one can say a word against you." She held out a hand to the younger girl. "Heart up, Liza—we will face the earl together."

The door of the room burst open, but it was not the earl who strode inside. Instead, there stood on the threshold a raffish-looking personage dressed in a bright blue coat, flowered purple waistcoat, mustard-colored breeches, and striped red stockings. Behind him skulked four equally unsavory-looking individuals.

"Beautiful ladies," crowed Barnaby White, "we meets at last."

Chapter Twelve

The fox had finally been viewed. The baying of hounds and Pardom's excited shouts could be heard in the near distance, obscured now by twilight darkness. But instead of joining in the chase, Sinclair slowed his horse.

He had not visited Pardom for more than a month, and harvest gold had long ago succeeded to November gloom. The earl's broad acreage lay fallow in the twilight, and there was the sting of sleet in the air. The dreary weather and dismal landscape recalled an old tag learned long ago in school.

" 'Now my life is in the sere,' " Sinclair mused aloud.

He broke off and rubbed absently at his right arm. His scars were aching in this raw, wet weather, as old wounds were wont to do. But in time men grew used to the scars they carried, and there was no use in regretting what might have been.

What future could there have been in a relationship that had begun in deceit and ended in attempted murder? Sinclair reminded himself that though Damaris had saved his life and probably the earl's as well, she had still brought Garland into their midst. Now she was back at Cardell House, and it was best to forget the distasteful incidents of the last month.

His lordship sighed. The trouble was that she seemed to have taken the sunlight with her.

Damaris Cardell had surprised him and amused him and exasperated him. She had made him want to laugh. It would be melodramatic to say that she had made him realize that life was sweet once more, but it was true that he now found his days as bleak as the November weather. And when he heard a husky voice or saw a flash of red hair, he felt a twist of memory that could be almost physically painful.

"Enough," Lord Sinclair said so forcefully that his horse laid back its ears.

He was a man of reason, a man of logic. He was no green youth mooning over a love affair gone sour. Even Liza seemed to have gotten over Garland—at least, she seemed pert enough this afternoon when she rode off to visit Miss Neece—and Pardom had been dropping broad hints that perhaps it was time that his nephew became leg-shackled to some suitable female and began his nursery. Perhaps for once, his uncle was right.

"Lord Sinclair! I say, sir!"

At the distant halloo, Sinclair turned his head and saw a youth with flaming red hair galloping toward him.

"Good God," Sinclair exclaimed. He spurred his own horse forward, meeting the boy at the foot of the hill. "What's happened to her?" he demanded.

Peter did not pretend to misunderstand. "Dami's gone to Carling. She didn't tell me why, but I think that Ambrose Garland's got something to do with it." He saw Lord Sinclair's expression and hastily held out Damaris's letter. "Here, sir. She wanted me to give this to the earl, but—"

Sinclair seized the letter, tore the envelope open, and scanned the contents. "Damnation," he exclaimed. "You don't mean that she went alone to Carling! Why didn't you go with her?"

Peter met the hard gray eyes without flinching. "Because she sent me here to find the earl—and you," he added after a moment.

Sinclair thought of Damaris pushing him out of the way of Garland's bullet. He thought of her nursing Pardom. He remembered the radiance of her smile. And now she was playing a dangerous game. For Liza's sake, she was going to put herself in Garland's power.

Sinclair pushed the letter back into Peter's hands. "I can't waste time explaining. Here, take this to my uncle. He's over the hill chasing a fox."

Then he wheeled his horse around and began to gallop toward Carling.

"Who are you? Leave the room at once," Liza gasped, then ducked behind Damaris as one of the ruffians drew a pistol from his belt and requested to know if Barnaby desired him to knock the gentry mort with the flash shap over the noddle.

"No, Spuddy, just you keep your ogles on 'em." White strolled into the room and went up to the unconscious form on the floor. He nudged it with his boot. "You, Mole. Go through 'is pockets and see if 'e 'as it on 'im."

A small, shriveled, pockmarked individual with the hardest eyes Damaris had ever seen scuttled forward, got down on one knee, and began to probe his pockets, which yielded nothing but a snuffbox, a silver watch, some sheets of paper, and a handful of small cash.

"Noffink," he announced. "No lurries an' no silver feeders neither."

White turned to Liza. "Where is it, ducks?"

"I don't know what you are talking about. How—how dare you address me in that common way?" Liza demanded indignantly.

"Oh, 'oity-toity, us 'as got a grand lady 'ere." White's yellow teeth were revealed in a disagreeable smile. "Wery well, yer 'ighnes. Where is yer fancy man's rolls of soft? Once we 'ave our fambles on what's ours, we'll part as friends."

"I don't know what you are talking about," Liza repeated.

"Might be we should search 'er," the one called Mole suggested. An evil glint flickered in his steely eyes as he looked Liza over.

"She has nothing and knows nothing," Damaris declared sternly. "She has no money and neither do I. Let us go at once."

"Feisty, ain't you, Red 'Air?" Barnaby White smiled again. "You look like a sensible 'ooman, so don't try and slumguzzle us. This cove 'ere owes me a lot of soft."

"I tell you," Damaris repeated, "we know nothing about any money."

The flat-faced ruffian called Spuddy pushed the pistol into Liza's face and threatened, "Quit trying to whiddle us, or I'll blow this one's noddle orf."

White pushed the pistol aside. " 'Old it, Spuddy. She was aiming to 'op the twig wif Garland. If she were his sweet'eart, she'd know where his money was. She just needs to be arsked friendly, like."

"If you lay a hand on us, I will scream the inn down," Damaris declared. "You may shoot us, but you will not get away with it. You will hang on Tyburn Tree."

It was a speech that Lord Tedell had made with

some effect in one of her books, but these ruffians seemed to regard it with great amusement.

"That's the barber," guffawed Spuddy. "Yell yer bloody noddle orf. Today's the sheepmen's market day, see, an' the inn is full to bustin' wif ale-blown coves. Uncommon full o' bounce, they are. They couldn't 'ear the last trump down there."

Another roar of laughter from downstairs, followed by a full-throated drinking song, gave the truth to this statement.

"Damaris, what are we going to *do*?" Liza moaned.

Grasping Liza's arm, Damaris attempted to rush for the door. Alone she might have escaped, but one of the ruffians caught Liza and pulled her back. Damaris went to the rescue and was caught, also. In desperation she kicked and clawed at her attacker, who swore violently and let her go.

"Help!" Damaris screamed. "Fire!"

A heavy hand clamped down on her mouth. "Do that again, an' I'll squeeze the puff outer you," the one called Spuddy threatened.

"Tie them up an' gag 'em," White counseled. "No use taking chances."

He aimed another kick at the recumbent Garland and sat down at a chair near the fire. "Since this barstid don't 'ave the soft, it's lucky we 'ave these females," he continued.

"I don't twig what your lay is, Barnaby," another confederate said, and was told to try and use his noddle instead of the windmills in his brain-box.

"The Earl of Pardom will pay to get 'is daughter back in one piece," White explained.

His henchmen looked at each other and grinned with delight until Mole demanded, "An' what if the bleeter don't pay up? There's talk that 'e ain't too keen on 'aving a daughter. Old sod wanted a son. Might be 'e won't fork over good soft for a female."

Even at such a moment, Damaris saw the pain in Liza's eyes. "Oh, 'e'll pay," White replied. An ugly look darkened his expression as he added, "Or else 'e won't know his daughter when 'e does get 'er back."

Liza sobbed, and spurred by this piteous sound, Damaris twisted her hands behind her. Once, Lord Tedell had been tied up by his enemies and had escaped sure death by loosening his bonds. She had researched this escape by having Peter tie her securely, and she had managed to wiggle free within an hour. But Peter had not tied such vicious knots, and besides, this was no game.

"What about this one?" Mole was asking, and Damaris felt White's eyes sidle around to her. They slimed over her skin like snails, leaving her feeling soiled. "She got a rich pa, too?"

The moneylender's lip curled. "No, Lord Sinclair 'as an eye for 'er. 'E'll pay for 'is fancy piece."

Damaris felt nausea at the pit of her stomach. Liza had begun to cry. The tears fell silently and slid into the gag that covered the rest of her face.

White walked over to the table, called for pen and paper, which one of his henchmen produced from a satchel he carried, and commenced to write. His confederates watched him admiringly.

"What's it say, Barnaby?" one of them asked after some time.

With a flourish White read, " 'To 'is lordship, the Earl of Pardom: Sir, we 'as your daughter. If you want to 'ave 'er back in as good a condition as when she left yer 'ouse, we respec'fully suggest you pay us ten thousand pound.' " He broke off to explain, "I've signed the note Ambrose Garland, so no one'll know it was us arsked for the ransom."

"Ten thousand quid," Mole repeated in an awed voice, and Spuddy added that he doubted that any man in his right mind would pay as much for a child's return.

"Well, the earl will. 'E's as rich as golden ball." White sealed his letter, adding, "Now I gots to write to that Lord Sinclair about Red 'Air 'ere. I ain't arsking as much for *'er*. No man alive'd pay more than a 'undred quid for 'is bit of muslin."

White chose one of his henchmen to deliver the ransom notes, warned him to repair directly to Pardom and then to ride to Lord Sinclair's Hampshire estates. "Make sure you puts this in a servant's 'and along wi' a gold sovereign as'll keep 'im from recergnizing you later on. We don't want their nibs to know who we are."

Damaris, who had been alternately seething and despairing as the letters were read, suddenly felt the rope that bound her hands give a little. She redoubled her efforts, twisting and wriggling her perspiration-slippery hands behind her back. *The game is not yet played out,* she told herself. *By now Peter must have reached the earl.*

Deliberately she did not let herself think of Lord Sinclair. As the despicable White had said, his lordship was in Hampshire. There was no reason why he should come through that door to rescue them.

Damaris shut her mind to wishful thinking and redoubled her efforts with her bonds, grateful that White and his ruffians had sat down at the table and were paying no attention to them.

"Now, we might as well be comfortable," White was saying expansively. "Nice of 'is nibs 'ere to pervide us with vittles. Dig right in, boys."

Ambrose Garland chose this moment to return to the world. He groaned, sat up, and put his hands to his head. "You struck me, you bitch," he groaned muzzily. Then he focused on White's face and groaned, "Oh, my God."

He closed his eyes again. "I'm going to be sick," he said.

For once, Damaris agreed with White, who said, "If you gets sick, you lies in yer mess. I ain't cleaning yew up, *Mr.* Garland. Now, there's a small matter of five thousand quid. That was the sum plus interest what you owed afore you 'opped the twig on us."

Garland began to stammer out excuses. "Shut up," White ordered. "If yew ain't got the money, yew ain't worth anything. Mole, take this cove someplace and cut 'is throat."

Mole rose with alacrity. "Let's not be hasty, White. I'm worth more to you alive than dead," Garland cried. "Look here, I know Pardom Hall like the back of my hand. And it is a *rich* estate."

"Are you saying that I'd slum some ken? Do you take me for a robber?" White demanded, outraged. "Never mind cutting 'is throat, Mole. Kill 'im gradual, like, for insinuating wicked things."

As Mole started toward Garland, he jumped to his feet and let fly with his fists. Mole went down, and White roared, "Shoot the barstid. What are you waiting fer?"

At that moment the bonds that held Damaris's wrists parted. She pulled her hands free, removed her gag, and untied Liza. No one was paying the slightest attention to them. They were all busy trying to subdue Garland.

Damaris clasped Liza's hand and motioned toward the door. Their footsteps masked by the noise of the fracas, the women slipped open the door and backed into the corridor. Then they closed the door behind them and sped down the long hall. They had almost reached the stairs when they heard heavy footsteps coming up.

"Oh, heavens," Liza wailed as they heard Spuddy's voice. "Damaris, we must hide!"

The door nearest them was locked. So was the door to the next chamber, but a stout walking stick had been set against the wall. Damaris snatched up the stick as she heard Spuddy exclaim, "I thought I 'eard your voices. Tryin' to 'op it, were you?"

Damaris shook her stick threateningly. "Keep your distance, or I shall hit you." To Liza she added urgently, "Run for it! Get help, Liza!"

"No, you don't. I 'ave me pistol set on you," Spuddy warned. "I will blow a 'ole through Red 'Air if you try and make a run for it, earl's daughter. Come along o' me peaceful, like, an' noffink will 'appen ter neither of yer."

Damaris cried, "Liza, don't believe him. Run!"

Liza looked mournfully at Damaris. "I cannot have him kill you," she groaned. "It is my fault that we are in the soup. Oh, Damaris, I am so *sorry*."

"Yew are going to be sorrier when Barnaby gets 'is fambles on you," threatened Spuddy as he dug his pistol in Damaris's ribs and marched them down the hall. He then pushed them into Mrs. Freddstick's parlor, announcing, " 'Ere is the lost sheep, Barnaby."

Damaris pulled free of Spuddy and boxed White's ears so hard that he staggered backward. At the same time she gave an earsplitting scream.

The door crashed open and Lord Sinclair stormed into the room. One blow felled White, another knocked Spuddy backward over the sofa and into Garland, who also fell to the floor.

Mole raised his weapon, but Liza flung a footstool at him. He tripped and fell, and next moment found himself seized by strong hands and flung halfway across the room.

"Oh, well *done*, Nicholas," Liza shouted, then as White retrieved the weapon Mole had dropped, added, "Be careful! That damned nail has got a pistol."

"Let me at 'em, curse it!"

Looking like a scarlet thunderbolt in his hunting coat, Pardom plunged into the room. He was followed by several stout footmen, grooms, and under-grooms. Jack, and a half dozen sheepmen and farmers in various stages of inebriation, brought up the rear.

White's pistol hand wavered. Lord Sinclair kicked it aside a second before the earl flung himself upon the moneylender and commenced beating him with his riding quirt.

For a few seconds there was chaos in the room. The earl continued to thrash White until that worthy begged to be allowed to surrender. He then tried to get his hands on Garland, who hastily ducked behind Jack. Some of the moneylender's henchmen managed to escape during the confusion, and these were pursued by grooms, footmen, and the more sober locals. Jack and a pair of red-nosed sheepmen busied themselves guarding the prisoners while Liza gathered up assorted weapons that had been discarded.

Amidst this confusion, Damaris found herself face-to-face with Lord Sinclair. The words with which she had meant to thank him for coming to their rescue died on her lips, and she spoke from the heart.

"I was so afraid," she told him. "I was afraid that you would not come."

Sinclair had intended to thank Damaris for her efforts on Liza's behalf. He had meant to keep his thanks courteous and cool, a little distant. But now that he was near her and she was gazing up at him with the dark eyes that had haunted his memory all these long weeks, his rehearsed speech took French leave.

Crying, "Are you sure you're not hurt?" he grasped her by the shoulders and gave her an ungentle shake. "You deserve to be, do you know that? Damaris, you were mad to come here alone."

He had worried about her. He cared for her safety. He did not altogether hate her or despise her. Damaris's eyes misted with irrepressible tears.

When she looked like that . . . Sinclair caught his breath. But before he could speak, Pardom bellowed, "Liza—there you are. Are you hurt, girl?"

Liza burst into tears and flung herself into the earl's arms. "Papa, I'm so fearfully sorry. I have been a blockhead."

The earl was visibly shaken. He had not realized until he had learned of Liza's disappearance how much he cared for the chit. In fact, since reading Damaris's hasty note, he had realized that if anything happened to his Liza, life would no longer be worth living. He held her close to him now and glared at Garland and White, who were being guarded by the sheepmen.

"I was the blockhead," he vowed unsteadily. "Arabella was right, curse it. If that villain there has hurt you, my—my dear, I'll strangle him with my bare hands."

"Before you do, there are a few points that need clearing up," Sinclair said. "Mr. Garland is going to confess to attempted kidnap and murder."

Garland looked up at this and snapped, "You have no proof."

Pardom clenched his riding quirt and stamped forward. "Let me have at that cur, Nicholas—let me, I tell you! Man was going to abduct my daughter."

"And he almost poisoned you, though actually, the gentleman had set out to feed *me* those poisonous mushrooms." Sinclair regarded Garland almost pleasantly. "You knew I had proof of your past activities, didn't you? You'd found a comfortable hiding place at Pardom and didn't want me to tell my uncle what I'd learned."

Garland's handsome face was marred by a sneer. Fury and desperation roughened his voice as he retorted, "Arrant nonsense. You can't prove your ridiculous accusations, Sinclair."

As if the man had not spoken, his lordship continued, "And it wasn't the first attempt you made on my life. I saw your face when you shot at me on the Carling road."

"How the devil could you have seen me? I was too far away for you to—" Garland checked himself too late. "You tricked me!"

"Wot in *'ell* is going on 'ere?"

Everyone turned at the new voice. A Junoesque lady clad in a dressing gown, slippers, and nightcap was standing in the doorway. A scent of onions, goose grease, and mustard plasters emanated strongly from her.

"I want to know," Mrs. Freddstick wheezed in a very nasal voice, "why an honesd woman can't get a wink of sleep in 'er own sickbed?" She swept the room with a furious look. "Wot are you lot doing in *my parlor*?"

Suddenly Garland made his move. Taking advantage of the momentary distraction, he pulled free from the sheepman who had him in custody, leaped across the room, and edged himself past Mrs. Freddstick. Sinclair lunged after him, but desperation lent wings to Garland's heels. As he bounded down the stairs, he encountered Nelly, the serving girl, coming up. Grasping her around the neck, he dragged her down the stairs with him.

"Let me go, or I'll break her neck," Garland threatened.

Sinclair hesitated on the stairs, and Garland hustled the terrified girl to the inn door. "Good-bye, my lord," he sneered. "I'll take leave of you now."

"No you won't," exclaimed a voice in a familiar rich contralto. "What?"

Garland turned his head, saw Miss Neece standing in the doorway, then yelped as he tripped over her outstretched foot. He stumbled, fell, and was up again—but by now Sinclair had reached him.

"So that's all right and tight," Miss Neece declared as his lordship immobilized the struggling Garland in a hammerlock. "I came just as soon as this redheaded lad—Peter's your name, ain't it?—rode up to Neece Place and asked whether Liza was with me. Of course, she wasn't. Used me as a red herrin'. Fact is, she'd come into town to see Miss Cardell."

The earl, who had descended the stairs with Liza and Damaris, looked startled before he realized that the inn's common room was full of eyes and ears. Scandal had to be quashed immediately if Liza's reputation was to survive.

"Nothin' more natural than Liza meetin' Damaris," Miss Neece continued in her impressive contralto. "They was friends. What? Grieved at bein' parted because of a misunderstandin'. Planned to take supper together. But no sooner had they met but these blackguards got hold of them and decided to hold them for ransom."

"Aha," the earl exclaimed. He was impressed at Arabella's logical explanation, and so, he was glad to note, were the other listeners. "So that was it."

Miss Neece strolled up to them and lowered her voice. "Time to get Liza home, Molyneux," she said. "Less said the better. What? Good thing I came when I did. *You*'d never have thought of a convincin' lie."

The earl's nod was almost humble. The thought of what could have happened to Liza had returned in full force, and he felt weaker than when he had consumed those unfortunate mushrooms.

He began to stammer his thanks, but Miss Neece waved these professions of gratitude aside. "Didn't do anythin' at all. What? Damaris is the one you should thank. If she hadn't kept her head, you'd have been beside the bridge."

She smiled at Damaris, winked, then put an arm around Liza. "Come," she declared, "I'm goin' back to Pardom with you. Don't worry about anythin', Molyneux. Leave it to me."

Everyone, even Lord Sinclair, watched with fascination as Miss Neece led Pardom and his daughter out the inn door. Pardom went meekly, and even the most inebriated of revelers drew back to give them respectful passage. They had recognized that Miss Neece had found a new Cause.

Damaris sat in Mrs. Freddstick's private parlor and waited for Peter to come back to the inn. She had seen him last when he had volunteered to help convey White and his henchmen to the watchtower, and that had been hours ago.

She wondered where he had got to and suspected that, flushed with triumph and excitement, her brother had joined the others in a victory toast somewhere. She wished that he would come, for it must be close to dawn, and her head was throbbing in spite of the tisane that Mrs. Freddstick had brewed with her own hands.

Mrs. Freddstick was elated with the arrest of so many scoundrels and considered Damaris courageous for squaring up to them. Not feeling at all brave, Damaris watched the still dark eastern sky and wanted nothing more than to go home.

As if in answer to her thoughts, the door creaked open. "It is high time you got here," Damaris exclaimed. "Do you know how late it is?"

"Very late," a deep voice replied agreeably.

Damaris whipped around as Lord Sinclair walked into the parlor and got up so quickly that she overturned her teacup. "What are you doing here?" she stammered.

"Making sure that it isn't *too* late." Sinclair closed the parlor door behind him. "I'm glad you are here. I was afraid that you would be on your way back to Kent."

"I am waiting for Peter." Damaris looked uneasily at the closed door. "I thought you had returned to Pardom with the others."

Sinclair shook his head. "I left the honors to Miss Neece. When last I saw them, she was telling Pardom exactly what he would say and do to quash even the hint of scandal. She went on to say that she was going to stay close for some time and make sure that Liza would be all right."

Miss Neece was definitely seizing the moment, Damaris thought. "What did the earl say?" she asked aloud

"He was quite meek. It won't last, of course," Lord Sinclair went on, "but hopefully what happened tonight has shaken some sense into Uncle Molyneux. He almost lost someone he loved more than all the world—as I myself nearly did."

He was talking about Liza, naturally. Damaris despised the weak-minded hope that stirred in her heart. She quelled it as ruthlessly as she had quashed the hopes and dreams that had blazed up when Lord Sinclair came storming through the door. Of course, he had come to rescue his cousin, no one else.

"What will happen to Mr. Garland now?" she wondered.

"He'll be brought before the magistrates. Let the law deal with him, and with White, too. Meanwhile, you and I have some unfinished business, ma'am. I've come to collect a debt."

She was bewildered. "But I have paid back the earl's hundred pounds."

"That's not what I meant. You've done me an injury."

"What could I have possibly done to you?" she cried.

"You've taken away what I hold most dear." Slowly Sinclair advanced toward Damaris, who repressed a hen-hearted desire to retreat before him. "You have bereft me of sleep, taken away my sunshine, and left me with no laughter, no warmth, no happiness."

He stopped, put out his hands, rested them lightly on Damaris's shoulders. "You've stolen my heart, Damaris."

The sound of her name on his lips was so sweet. So was his touch. Damaris knew in that moment that she still loved Lord Sinclair and would probably love him till the day she died. The ache in her heart intensified as she remembered what Barnaby White had said about Lord Sinclair thinking of her as his fancy woman.

A man like Lord Sinclair would not make an honorable proposal to someone he considered an adventuress, so his lordship was no doubt giving her a slip on the shoulder. Due to her past actions, he probably thought that she would welcome improper advances.

It was time to correct that mistake. Damaris looked him squarely in the eye as she said, "Lord Sinclair, I will not be your bit of muslin. The Cardells are good family, and— Oh, do stop laughing in that odious manner. How dare you offer me carte blanche?"

Sinclair stopped her flow of talk by kissing her firmly. Perhaps she had no morals at all, Damaris thought dreamily, for at the touch of his lips, all reason and righteous indignation disappeared. It was as though the night was suddenly over and a bright and beautiful day was dawning.

"This is the second dawn we have seen together," Sinclair murmured against her cheek. "The last time this happened, you left Pardom and me, and I let you go because I was a fool. But even a fool can learn. Marry me, Damaris."

Marry.

Like a rose petal falling, the word drifted gently down until it lay in Damaris's heart. But almost instantly there was another doubt.

"Oh, Nicholas, are you sure you are not saying this from gratitude? Because of my trying to rescue Liza?"

For answer, he kissed her again, kissed her so thoroughly that she could not breathe, kissed her with such single-minded concentration and passion that the air around them seemed to singe and smolder. Damaris surrendered. She clung to him and kissed Lord Sinclair back as though she could never have enough of the touch and feel and taste of him.

They stayed fused together until the universe seemed to cartwheel around them and dark spots caused by lack of oxygen danced before their eyes. Then, finally, reluctantly, they drew apart, breathing raggedly and clinging to each other for support.

"Do you still think I want to marry you out of gratitude?" Lord Sinclair demanded huskily.

Damaris drew in a much-needed breath. "If only I could be sure—"

He would have kissed her again, but the troubled note in her voice checked him. "What is it that worries you?" he asked quietly.

"I am not sure whether you will approve of what I wish to do. Nicholas, I have realized that I do not write simply to pay bills but because I enjoy it. I want to go on writing, but not about Lord Tedell."

"And so?" Sinclair prompted as she broke off.

"I want to write a book with a woman as the central character. Lady Penelope will be a brave woman with a clever mind and a gentle, loyal heart."

"She reminds me of someone close to me," Sinclair murmured.

Damaris misunderstood. "I think," she said earnestly, "that I am going to make her more than a little like Miss Neece. And since it would be a pity to waste all this research, I would like to base the novel on tonight's events at the Silver Snail."

Sinclair gave a shout of laughter. Then he sobered. "I'm not such a fool as to think I can order you about or govern your life. Write what you choose, Madam Mystery. I make only one small condition."

"A condition, Nicholas?"

"Call it a request in the interests of self-preservation." Clasping his arms firmly around Damaris, Sinclair smiled down into her upturned face. "From now on, sweetheart, *don't* involve me in any more of your research."